D0236325

DANCING PEEL

DANCING PEEL

by

LORNA HILL

Illustrated by Anne Grahame Johnstone

AWARD PUBLICATIONS LIMITED

ISBN 0-86163-838-7

Text copyright Lorna Hill 1954
Illustrations copyright © Award Publications Limited 1997

First published 1954 by Thomas Nelson and Sons Ltd
This edition first published 1997
Second impression 2003

Published by Award Publications Limited,
27 Longford Street, London NW1 3DZ

Printed in Singapore

All rights reserved

CONTENTS

Part One: Winter

1   THE PEEL-TOWER

In case you have never seen an old Northumbrian peel-tower, I will tell you what Dancing Peel was like. It was quite a large building, built of huge, rough blocks of grey stone, and it stood at the northern end of Mintlaw, ten miles on the English side of the border. There were no windows on its north side because, when it was built, windows were danger spots. It was from the north that danger came.

The south windows of the peel looked out over a low drystone wall bounding the garden, and then to the village green. Each morning a line of ducks belonging to Heatherside Farm waddled over the grass and dropped with a plop into the brown, peaty Mintlaw burn. In the evening, back they would waddle, more slowly because now they were full of worms. Over by the churchyard wall, old Sarah Dodd's cow grazed peacefully on a menu of butter-cups, cowslips, bedstraw, with a root or two of meadowsweet thrown in for good measure. No won-der her butter was yellow and sweet-scented! On the weathercock which topped the tiny church steeple a family of rooks sat and preened themselves with dignity. At the door of one of the cottages, a cat with a family of kittens purred loudly in an ecstasy of warmth and well-being.

This picture is of the peel in summertime, which comes late to Northumberland and departs early. In winter, it was different. In the dark days of December and January, and February too, the skies drew down over the old fortress until the clouds, heavy with snow, seemed almost to touch its scarred walls and battlements. Outside, snowdrifts piled up higher than your head, icicles hung from the mouths of the gargoyles round the roof, and the old grey stones were covered with ice. Outside, the north wind howled across the moorland. Inside, it keened through the stone passages and bellowed in the chimneys, making those within shudder and run for the snugness of the Round Lounge, which was the only room in the peel that was ever really warm in wintertime.

From the flat roof of the peel you could see the miles and miles of Border country. A wild, empty place you may say, but the people who lived there didn't think so. They loved every inch of their ancient Border stronghold and its surroundings.

Dancing Peel had originally been a fortified manor-house, built in 1214. In 1500, or thereabouts, the parts still standing had been made into one of those strange buildings one finds in dozens on the

Border – a peel-tower. Exactly when it became the vicarage nobody knew.

The vicar in those olden days must have been tough indeed! In one ancient record it was set down that the vicar was forbidden to carry arms in church, other than a stout stick. What were the authorities afraid of? That their vicar might carry out a few Border raids on his own account?

The last vicar to live in the peel-tower was a certain Edmond François Dancy – originally d'Ancy – whose family had escaped from France during the Revolution. It was from Mr Dancy that the Dancy children got their names and their love of the ballet. After all, didn't ballet begin at the court of Louix XIV of France? It certainly couldn't have been from their mother, a Northumbrian farmer's daughter. Poor Mrs Dancy! She must have had a hectic life with her temperamental husband and their two temperamental children. As for herself, she was as calm and unruffled as Corbie Lough on a still June day.

In order to add to his small income, Mr Dancy had taken to writing books about Church history – as dull as ditchwater his children thought them! But even books as dull as ditchwater are bought by some people, it seems, because, although Mr Dancy's weren't what you might call bestsellers, they did bring in a few royalties each year, and every little helped.

When Mr Dancy died, leaving his family totally unprovided for except for a tiny pension and the royalties from his books, Mrs Dancy's farming background came to the rescue. She had always kept poultry, and she now increased her stock until she had quite a nice little chicken-farm. Her children, Maximilian and Annette, weren't a great deal of help to her, though. They made pets of the chickens and ducks, and when Christmas came, and the birds had to go to market, you'd have thought there had been a death in the family! All the same, the children were glad enough of the extra money. Because of the 'egg money' they were able to have Bella to help in the peel, and scrub out the cool dairies and storerooms. It was the egg money that paid for Annette's ballet classes, and Max's fencing lessons. He took to fencing like the proverbial duck to water, and was Junior County Fencing Champion in no time.

Max's full name was Maximilian Leopold Duchène Dancy. He was seventeen, slim and dark, with a thin, proud face, black eyes, and a haughty nose. His hands were slender and expressive, and he used them to make his meaning clear upon every possible occasion. He went to the Royal Grammar School in Newcastle, and it is hardly to be wondered at that his best subject – not counting fencing – was languages. Even in this, it must be admitted that his report said: 'More flowery than accurate!' However, he had won a travelling scholarship last summer holidays, and had gone to Italy and Germany to study languages, but had ended up in Spain where he studied not only the language but also the guitar and art of Spanish dancing. Nowadays, the old peel-tower echoed to the sound of strings gently plucked, the click of the castanets, the shouts of '*olé*!' and the stamp of feet as Max practised.

If Max couldn't remember certain bars of music he'd heard he'd hold his aching head and groan, 'I cannot remember that music. There is a gap, and I cannot remember . . .'

Mrs Dancy would stroke his black hair and murmur reassuringly: 'I expect if you stop worrying about it, it will come, Max dear.'

And sure enough, later on that evening, a radiant

Max would burst into the kitchen where Mrs Dancy was making a pudding for that night's dinner and announce triumphantly, 'You were right! I remembered those bars, it goes like this . . . Dance with me, Mother! Oh, but of course you can't. The pudding would suffer!'

'You needn't say it like that!' his mother would reply. 'You'll be glad enough to eat it when the time comes!'

But Max would already have gone back to the cold storeroom, which had once been the solar, or sitting-room, and which Max had taken for his own use, and where he kept himself warm by dancing. The windows were pointed at the top like those in a chapel, and the roof was ornamented with faded blue and gold stars. There was a coat of arms over the hooded fireplace, together with a fascinating row of stone images.

Well, now we come to the member of the Dancy family that this story is most about, Annette Eugénie Mathilde Dancy. She was usually called by the first of these names, except by Angus who called her – no, I'm not going to tell you what Angus called her, although he had every excuse for doing so! I won't tell you anything about Angus here, either. We'll meet him later on.

Annette was not beautiful, she wasn't even pretty. She had enormous dark eyes, much too large for her pale little face, and a large, generous mouth to match. Her hair was black, and cut across her forehead in a fringe. Underneath the fringe, it fell straight to her shoulders. Nothing you could do would make Annette's hair curl even the least little bit. When she plaited it and pinned it on top of her head for her ballet classes, she looked all eyes. The other thing you noticed about Annette was that she had long thin legs, and arms equally skinny. She used to sigh over her skinniness, but Miss Brandon, her dancing-mistress, didn't seem to share her anxiety.

'You'd far better be on the thin side, Annette,' she would say. 'You can always fill out, but you can't take off – especially the thighs.' Now, the thighs are an awful danger-spot. More dancers have been turned down by the best ballet companies on account of too well-covered thighs than for almost any other reason. Annette was as keen on dancing as her brother, and was quite determined to be a ballet dancer when she grew up.

Now the only other thing to explain is how the Dancy family went on living in the peel-tower after their father died, and how it came to be called Dancing Peel. The new vicar was a bachelor of about sixty, and he refused to live in 'that mouldering old ruin'. He declared he'd rather live in a two-roomed cottage in the village, while the Dancys went on living in the peel, for which they paid a small rent.

In time, the vicar's cottage was referred to as 'The Vicarage', while the peel-tower was called Dancy Peel, and it wasn't long before this became Dancing Peel.

2 DANCING-SCHOOL

The egg money didn't run to boarding-schools, so the young Dancys went to school in Newcastle. They stayed at the flat of an old school friend of their mother whom they called Aunt Molly but who was really no relation to them at all.

In summertime Max and Annette went home most weekends, but in the winter, when the road was piled high with snowdrifts, they stayed all the time with Aunt Molly. This was an excellent opportunity for attending nightly ballet classes, fencing lessons, and Spanish dance practice. The egg money didn't really run to all this either, but Annette had come to a business arrangement with Miss Brandon. She helped with the little ones on Saturday mornings during the winter, and with the Grade Fives on Tuesday evenings, in return for her own classes. Max spent two evenings a week baby-sitting, which paid for his one ballet class a week with Miss Brandon, and also for the hire of a small room on two other nights where he and other Spanish dancing enthusiasts practised.

Sometimes Annette joined them. On one evening a week the two of them went to the Tyneside Ballet Workshop, where they took small parts in the ballets – children, animals, and so on. Sometimes Max got a solo, because Spanish dancing was a novelty. At their next show, he hoped to do a Spanish number with Annette as his partner. Annette, with her black hair and large dark eyes, made up well as a Spanish dancer. All the same, Annette didn't really want to be a Spanish dancer. Her feelings were all towards ballet proper. With this in mind, she was taking her first major RAD exam – the Elementary – in the autumn. In between all this dancing, the two children were working hard at school. But after school, their real life began. Annette would snatch up her canvas bag stuffed with ballet shoes and tights, hop on a bus at the school gates to Rothbury Crescent, where she would drop off at the corner. White letters on the fanlight of a building announced THE ELEANOR BRANDON SCHOOL OF DANCING.

On this particular evening, Annette arrived later than usual. Already, on the far side of the double glass doors, the place was fairly humming with activity. Every room was crowded. Children tap-dancing, grown-ups ballroom dancing, ballet students running round in tights and tunics, hair neatly plastered back with nets and bandeaux, their blocked shoes tap-tapping on the polished floors. As doors opened and shut, snatches of cool, clipped voices reached her ears . . . 'Chassé – half-turn – close – chassé – sway –

drop. Again, please.' Sounds of pianos playing hot stuff for the tappers and RAD examination music for the ballet students . . . '*Développé* – one, and two, and three, and four, and – Hold it, Julia! More turned out, Rosemary. One, and two, and –'

Even the dressing-rooms were full to overflowing. Annette made for the Junior Students' cloakroom and put her head round the door. Nobody took the slightest notice of her. Everyone was far too busy. A crowd of schoolchildren, in every stage of dress and undress, eating sandwiches, cakes, fruit, drinking out of bottles and flasks; sitting on tables darning ballet-shoes and tights; reading ballet magazines. Yet more children, drawn a little apart, busily doing their homework for school next day, with Annette now among them.

Suddenly the door opened and a fresh batch of girls, panting and laughing, crowded in. One of the biggest of the newcomers swept off her net bandeau in a graceful gesture, letting her mane of fair hair ripple over her shoulders.

'Time for the Elementaries!' she announced. 'Miss Brandon says will you be *quick*. The classes are already twenty minutes behind time. By the way, there's *someone* in there – in the big studio. So take care!'

The effect of her words was magical. Someone? There might be nothing in the rumour – ballet schools are full of rumours, most of them false. Carol was probably pulling everyone's leg, and there'd be no one in the big studio at all, or perhaps a new

16

pianist. Or if there was an onlooker, it would turn out to be somebody's mother! On the other hand, you never knew – the stranger *might* be a talent scout.

'Carol, are my tights straight?'

'Julia, you're sitting on my case and it's got my tunic in. I washed and ironed it specially for the show we're doing on Saturday but I think I'll wear it tonight. You never know.'

'Annette Dancy! What on *earth* are you doing up there?'

'I'm – trying – to – get – that – box – down,' panted Annette from where she was perched on the top of a high cupboard where all the costumes from the Brandon School shows were kept. 'If – only – you – people – would – get – out – of – the – way. It's got my best point-shoes in. I keep them there for safety.'

Alas! The shoes might be safe, but poor Annette wasn't! There was an ominous creaking of wood, a sound of splintering, an awful moment when dancer and cupboard swayed backwards and forwards together in a sort of mad war-dance. Then a sickening crash.

'Oh, Annette! Are you all right?'

A wail came from underneath a pile of Hungarian peasant costumes which had been shot out of their boxes on to the floor.

'Annette, what's the matter? Are you hurt?'

'It's my *eye*, I caught it on the edge of the cupboard. It's my eye!'

Well, an eye with sticking-plaster over it and a nose

with a large scratch down one side oughtn't to prejudice one's chances as a ballet-dancer. Be that as it may, the sad fact remained that the someone in the big studio *did* happen to be Someone Terribly Important. She was from the Royal Ballet School, as a matter of fact, and she chose the two best of Miss Brandon's pupils for the two vacant places in the school for the next year. Annette Dancy wasn't one of them.

'Cheer up, dear,' Miss Brandon said bracingly. 'You can go to an audition in London, you know. Another chance will come.'

'N-not l-like this one!' hiccoughed poor Annette. 'It w-was the c-chance of a l-lifetime. You *know* it w-was, Miss B-Brandon. I m-might have g-got in if she'd seen me – I mean my n-nose – at my b-best, but in London, along with millions of other k-kids, I w-won't stand an earthly.'

'I don't think you'd have stood an earthly anyway,' said Miss Brandon candidly. 'You're not advanced enough yet, you know – not for the Senior School which is where you would have to go. You started a little late. How old were you when you began to learn ballet, Annette?'

'I w-was t-twelve.'

'It's a year too late,' declared Miss Brandon. 'But never mind, you'll catch up, and there are other schools in London in connection with ballet companies which don't demand quite such a high standard. You can start in one of them.'

'But they're not the Royal Ballet School,' said

19

Annette, drying her eyes on somebody's tights that were hanging on the back of a chair.

'Lots of people have got from the Ballet Rambert, for instance, into one of the Royal Ballet companies,' said Miss Brandon wisely. 'Then there's the Cosmopolitan Ballet School, run in conjunction with their excellent company, small though it is. We'll get you into that. You'll see!'

Annette collected up her belongings and caught the bus home. Happily, she soon forgot all about her misfortune and was practising harder than ever. For one thing, it was only three weeks to half-term, and she and Max would be going home for a long weekend. Spring was almost here, and soon the larks and the curlews would be calling on the moors round Dancing Peel.

3   NEWS!

One day, soon after that dancing class, a letter arrived at Aunt Molly's flat which told Annette and her brother that something had happened which might very well change their whole lives. Mrs Dancy wrote to say that old Mr Matthew Collingwood, the aged vicar of Mintlaw, had died in his sleep.

My darlings, said the letter.

We have all had a very great shock. Poor old Mr Collingwood was found dead in his bed when Nancy Carr went in to get his breakfast as usual this morning. The doctor says his heart has been in a bad way for a long time, but nobody knew. Of course, he was over sixty when he came here, and that was ten years ago. I suppose he couldn't be expected to live for ever. But I can't yet believe that he has really gone, that I shan't ever see him walking into the little church again, or down the village street. It seems impossible! I think the villagers will miss him greatly, dear old man. He was always so ready to share their troubles.

Now apart from the personal shock of losing a very dear friend, Mr Collingwood's death may affect us greatly as a family. As you know, our peel-tower is really the vicarage, and it is more than probable that the new vicar will want to live in it. In fact, I don't see where else he can live – especially if he is married and has a family. In any case, he can't live in old Mr Collingwood's cottage because it is already condemned, and will be pulled down now that he is gone. So you see how it is, darlings. I thought I had better warn you! I will let you know the moment there is any news.

With all my love,
Mummy.

P.S. How is your poor, bruised eye, Annette? And the nose, too? Try some arnica ointment on the bruise. It's very good.

'Oh, Max!' wailed Annette. 'We couldn't – we *couldn't* leave Dancing Peel. Why, it's our home!'

'It looks as if we shall have to,' said Max gloomily. 'The new vicar is sure to want to live in the peel. Who wouldn't?'

During the next two weeks, no less than three clergymen came to look at the living of Mintlaw, shook their heads, and went away again. It wasn't the smallness of the stipend; it wasn't the remoteness of the village; it wasn't even the big, scattered parish and the difficulty of visiting the people in it. No, it was the ancient weather-beaten peel-tower-cum-vicarage.

Mrs Dancy pointed out that you could get the Round Lounge passably warm if you got in a good store of logs before winter set in, and piled them on the open fire unstintingly. She added that the spiral stone staircase leading to the north wing was really most economical, because you couldn't carpet it, however much you wanted to, and the same applied to the kitchen – you couldn't put anything on the flagged floor because it rotted immediately. The architect said it had something to do with a spring that ran underneath in the dungeon, and never dried up. Oh, yes, there was a dungeon underneath the kitchen! No, of course there wasn't any truth in the story that if you left anything on the kitchen table for a few minutes – a new loaf of bread, for instance – when you returned it had vanished. There was no ghost at Dancing Peel, only the rats. They came up from the old part of the building at nights, but you never actually saw them – unless you came down for anything. Sometimes Bella wondered if Mrs Dancy was turning the visitors 'agin the peel a-purpose like'.

And then it happened!

Darlings, wrote Mrs Dancy.

A new vicar – a Mr MacCrimmon – has been appointed. He has two children, it seems, and he is going to be here to take the Easter services. He is used to out-of-the-way places, because he has just come from Portree, in the Island of Skye . . .

'Max!' cried Annette, trying to snatch the letter out of her brother's hands. 'What about us? What about Dancing Peel? Does she say where the new vicar is going to live?'

'Give me time!' begged Max. 'I'm just coming to that bit. Where was I? Oh yes . . . *Island of Skye, where there's an English church, so he wasn't a bit dismayed at the idea of the vicarage being in a peel-tower . . .*'

'Then he does want to live in it!' burst out Annette. 'I knew it! I knew he would! The old beast!'

'He's not old,' corrected Max solemnly. 'Mother says, here, he's in early middle-age. That means about forty-five, I suppose. And I don't believe he's beastly.'

'He must be. No one but a beastly person would want to turn us out of our home.'

'It's *his* home by rights,' said Max. 'You must remember that, Annette.'

'Yes, but he hasn't been living in it for years and years. He can't love it as we do,' said Annette, bursting into tears.

'Will you please shut up, Annette, and let me finish the letter. Mother says that Mr MacCrimmon hated the idea of turning us out of what had come to be our home, so he wouldn't dream of living in it.'

'Oh, Max! Why didn't you say so before? I've been suffering agonies . . .'

'You didn't give me a chance.'

'Well, where *is* he going to live?' asked Annette, drying her tear-streaked face on the end of Aunt Molly's tablecloth. 'In the belfry?'

'No,' said Max seriously. 'In the Lodge.'

'The Lodge? But it hasn't any roof!'

'If you would stop talking for just half a minute,' put in Max, 'I might get the rest of the letter read.' His eye ran swiftly down the page. 'Mother says that the new vicar is a relative of the Coldburn Hall people – Sir William's cousin, or something. They're going to take a roof off one of the outbuildings at the Hall, and put it on the Lodge, and a lot of the timber is to come off the estate, too, so –'

25

But Annette wasn't listening. She had put her head down on Max's knee and was once more sobbing wildly, and it was just at this moment that Aunt Molly herself appeared.

'It's all right, Aunt Molly,' sobbed Annette. 'I h-haven't been exp-pelled, or anything! I'm crying because I'm so terribly, terribly h-happy!'

4 HALF-TERM

Annette never knew how she managed to live through the long Friday afternoon that next week. She couldn't think of anything except that it was half-term, that she was going home to Dancing Peel, and that it was spring!

She flung on her clothes all anyhow and was pulled up by a prefect who pointed out that she had got her hat on back-to-front and her coat done up on the wrong buttons.

'What does anything matter today? It's half-term, and I'm going home.'

'It matters a lot,' said the prefect. 'You'll let down the school.'

'I shall miss the bus in another minute,' retorted Annette, 'and that will be lots worse. Oh, bother! Now I've forgotten my shoes.'

Eventually she found one of them under a wash-basin and the other in her shoe-bag, where she had absent-mindedly put it that morning. Tidiness wasn't one of Annette's virtues. Finally she shot out of the school gates with just over five minutes to catch the bus. She managed it with ten seconds to spare.

There it stood, the country bus, waiting to carry its passengers back to their homes – lonely farms with only muddy cart-tracks for roads, shepherds' huts standing alone, miles from anywhere, gamekeepers' cottages at the foot of gloomy drives of country mansions, Border peel-houses and towers like her own, and finally a small, grey village tucked away in a fold of the moors.

The bus was crammed to the very doors and people were sitting on all sorts of things, even on each other's laps! Several schoolboys were crouched on the floor at the back. An old shepherd, with his dog and crooked stick, occupied an upturned box beside the driver. A farmer's wife, with a large basket cheeping with chickens, shared a seat with three interested children. In the gangway, a row of women who had been shopping swayed to and fro as the bus careered up the Great North Road. Several men leaned against the door. Max was among them, one hand clutching the handle, the other thrust into his coat-pocket from whence issued strange clicking noises, made, Annette knew, by a pair of castanets! Max was never parted from them.

'Tak a seat, hinny!'

Annette turned round, not without difficulty. A large farmer had pulled a sack of seed potatoes out from underneath a seat and was warmly inviting her to sit upon it.

'I feel like a hen brooding a clutch of eggs,' she laughed, as she accepted the invitation.

It had been an exceptionally hard winter. Indeed it was afterwards referred to as 'the year of the great storm', but now it was March and there were no signs of snow in the Newcastle streets. But as the bus left the town there were signs all right. To be sure, the fields were green, but the sides of the road were still banked with snow, quite high in places. In the distance you could see the Rothbury Heights capped with snow.

Annette remembered her mother's letters about the storm at Mintlaw. How the village had been cut off for weeks, and letters had had to be taken to Bellingham by 'Billy-the-Postie' on horseback. It was a good thing Billy was a countryman and a good rider! The village ran short of most things. As soon as the gangs of men had dug out the road, the Arctic snow-laden wind, blowing across the moors, had filled it in again. Hundreds of sheep had perished in the district, and more than one old shepherd died of exposure looking for them. Things had become so bad that a huge fire was kept burning in the village school, and everyone gathered there to do their cooking, discuss the weather, and keep warm. At dusk, about four o'clock, they had just gone to bed as there were no lights. Yes, it had indeed been a hard winter – the worst in living memory, people said.

By the time the bus had reached Whinsheil it was dark, but Max and Annette didn't mind. They were country children, and a walk of three or four miles along a lonely country road, with only the stars to light them, didn't dismay them. After the smoke and fumes of Newcastle, the pure, cold air was like wine. The moon rose and shone with ghostly radiance on peak and crag crowned with snow. The sides of the road were banked high with icy mounds, but the moorland burns, splashing merrily and glittering in the moonlight, told that the iron hand of frost had loosened, and spring was coming.

'Whatever are you dreaming about, Annette?' shouted Max. 'I've asked you three times whether you want to go and see Teresa and Luisillo at the Theatre Royal next week. Gallery, of course.'

'Naturally I want to go,' said Annette. 'Though I'd rather it was the ordinary ballet.'

'Ordinary ballet?' echoed Max. 'What's ballet compared with a Flamenco gipsy dance? You should have seen –'

'I know! Those gipsies you ran into in Alhambra –'

Max rose to the bait as Annette intended. 'They were artistes, every one of them!' he said. Then he laughed. 'Hello! Here we are at the old crossroads. This is where they strung 'em up on the gibbet – cattle-thieves, rustlers, moss-troopers, parsons – all the lot! No discriminating in those days! Many a man has hung here on a still, frosty, starlight night like tonight, creaking, groaning in his chains –'

'Be quiet, you horrid boy!' cried Annette, putting her hands over her ears. 'I don't believe a word of it!'

'It's quite true,' insisted Max. 'You've only to read your history book, but of course you never do. You're always far too busy with your entrechats and battements.'

'What about you and your zapateados, and your sevillanas?' retorted Annette.

'Granted!' agreed Max, with a click of his castanets. 'But I *do* leave room for a little local history.'

'By the way,' said Annette, abruptly changing the subject, 'did Mummy say in her letter whether Mr MacCrimmon, the new vicar, was married?'

'Must be,' said Max. 'Didn't I tell you – there are two kids.'

'He might be a widower,' said Annette. 'I hope he isn't, though. He's sure to have spoilt the kids and they'll be awful, and scream whenever they want anything. We'll have a dreadful job keeping them in their place.'

It was nearly eight o'clock when they crossed the last stretch of moorland that lay between them and Mintlaw. They were taking short cuts over the moor, paths known only to the inhabitants of the district, and they sang as they walked.

'I'm hungry,' Annette said, as the roofs of Mintlaw appeared over the top of a snowy hillside. 'Had no time for even a biscuit.'

'I've got half a bar of chocolate somewhere,' Max said, rummaging in his pockets, 'if only I could find it . . . Oh, here it is. Afraid it's a bit the worse for

wear, though. It's got mixed up with some string.'

Annette accepted the chocolate gratefully. Even if it *had* melted, and was now more string than chocolate, it tasted delicious if you sucked it.

'It will spoil your supper, of course, so don't guzzle the lot. Mother will be hurt if you can't eat the whopper of a meal she's sure to have ready for us.'

Annette licked her fingers regretfully and put the sticky mess back in Max's pocket.

'All right,' she said. She was tired and happy, and in a frame of mind to agree to anything.

As they made their way up the overgrown drive that led to the peel they passed the Lodge, a picturesque old cottage built by a former vicar in the days when the younger son of the squire entered the Ministry as a matter of course, and of course had a private income. The Lodge was meant to house the coachman or the gardener. Later it had housed all sorts of different people who paid a small rent of a few shillings a week, and this was used to augment the vicar's tiny income. In recent years, however, the roof of the Lodge had fallen in, and it had not been repaired as the authorities said it would cost more than it was worth.

Tonight, the Lodge looked grim and forsaken. Its slateless roof yawned like, as Annette put it, 'a mouth without any teeth'. Its curtainless windows looked like sightless eyes gazing out blindly on a cold, bleak world.

'Ugh!' said Annette with a shiver. 'It's eerie! I don't believe he's really going to live there – the new vicar, I mean.'

But she was wrong. When the two children flung themselves down in a couple of easy chairs in the Round Lounge before the roaring log fire, they heard that already work had begun on the Lodge.

'At least,' amended Mrs Dancy, 'the architect has been here with the plans, and the estate men are to begin on Monday.'

'Mummy,' said Annette, wriggling her cold toes in the heat of the fire, 'Mummy, what are the children like? You said there were two, didn't you?'

'I don't know the least thing about them,' confessed Mrs Dancy, 'except that there's a boy and a girl. Poor little things, we must be very kind to them. They have no mother, you see –'

'I knew it!' burst out Annette. 'I said so, didn't I, Max? I said their father would be a widower with two horrible, spoilt little brats –'

'Annette!' reproved Mrs Dancy.

'Sorry, Mummy, but it's true, isn't it? Lone fathers always spoil children. You've often said so yourself. But it doesn't really matter. They'll be in the Lodge, and as long as they stay there and don't bother us, I shan't mind.'

An odd expression came over Mrs Dancy's face, but she said no more. Bella had appeared with a tray laden with all the things Annette and Max loved best, and perhaps Mrs Dancy thought that widowers' children weren't the only spoilt ones . . .

'Home-fed sausage and mashed potato,' exclaimed Max blissfully.

'And trifle with real farmhouse cream on it,' said Annette. 'Three cheers for home!'

'There's plenty more i' the kitchen if ye can eat it,' said Bella, her round red face beaming like the rising sun. She liked having the children at home.

They settled down to their supper, and for a long time neither of them said a word. The flames of the log fire flickered on the uneven floor and low raftered ceiling of the old room; on the deep window seats built into the thickness of the walls; on the narrow slit-like window by the side of the fireplace, where, in times past, the warlike owners of the peel-tower used to keep watch, day after dangerous day. By means of this spy-hole they could see through a window in the old kitchen, and thence through a slit in the outer wall which surrounded the peel, away to a dark gap in the rolling hills where the Scots would come riding on their murderous raids.

Mrs Dancy never thought about these things, though she loved her home dearly; but Annette would many a time climb up to the flat roof and look down at the brown Mintlaw burn sighing among its rushes, and hear the curlews calling as they wheeled overhead.

5   AN ENCOUNTER

You might have thought that, living in the depths of the country, the Dancy children would be taught to ride almost before they could walk, and handle a fishing-rod to the manner born. The fact was that, although they were both passionately fond of the country itself, they hated the sporting side of country life. They couldn't bear to think of timid hares being chased to death. Neither did they see the fun of rearing glossy-winged pheasants and motherly partridges for the pleasure of shooting them down during a few days' 'sport'. As for fishing – they liked to see the fish swimming about in the Mintlaw burn better than on the end of a fisherman's rod.

Then there was fox-hunting. When Annette read in the paper about a man who had given the hunted fox asylum in a cricket pavilion, her heart rejoiced and she wished a poor fox would take refuge in their peel-tower!

On Saturday morning Annette was up early. Out of her bedroom window she could see a glint of yellow between the trees, and she knew that the crocuses were in bloom. Flower-loving Mr Dancy had planted the bulbs in hundreds in all the sunniest places round his home, and now, as the snow retreated, the crocuses took possession and covered the ground with a carpet of gold.

She dressed quickly, anxious not to waste a moment of her precious holiday, and went out into the corridor. She shivered. The icy cold of winter still lingered in the massive stone walls of the peel, though outside the wind was warm. In the autumn exactly the opposite happened. Long after the snow was falling outside the warmth of summer remained in the old house.

Annette threw up her head and sniffed like a dog. Whenever she came home she was met by the special smell of the peel, that smell which is made up of stone, paraffin oil, wood fires and general antiquity, and is peculiar to churches and old buildings.

Before taking a short cut down the spiral staircase, Annette glanced into her brother's room. He was still fast asleep, and she hadn't the heart to wake him. He lay with one slim foot hanging out from underneath the bedclothes. His hands, strong and supple as steel through much castanet playing, lay on top of the quilt, blue veined, with the delicate bones showing through the thin skin. Suddenly it occurred to Annette that, even when he was asleep, you would have known that Max was a Spanish dancer. All the pride and arrogance of Spain was written on his handsome, finely cut features. It was the same with other people, she thought. When they looked after animals, they got to resemble those animals. Bella, for instance. Bella's mild brown eyes were just like those of the patient cows she milked on her smallholding.

'Me, too,' added Annette, glancing at herself complacently in Max's looking-glass as she passed. 'You'd know I was a ballet-dancer.' There was no vanity in her thoughts. She wasn't admiring herself – no one could have cared less than Annette what she looked like, upon ordinary occasions, but it *did* please her that the dark-eyed, dark-haired girl in the looking-glass might have been any one of a hundred ballet-dancers, past or present. Even the fair-haired ones have the same look, stamping them for what they are.

She went down to the kitchen. It faced east, and a flood of sunlight was streaming through the two deep-set, square windows and lying in warm pools on the flagged floor, polished by Bella until it shone like a wet lake. The old wooden farmhouse table was scrubbed to a dazzling whiteness. Bella would have scorned a modern one . . . On the 'hookie' mat, in front of the big open fireplace, crouched Rob Roy, the Dancy cat, wearing a very disgruntled expression on his dignified features. He looked round expectantly as the door opened. Here at last was someone to light his fire! But Annette wasn't thinking about fires. Cutting a large, thick slice off a loaf of Bella's home-made bread and buttering it, she let herself out of the back door, hurried across a small cobbled courtyard, through a further door, then through a closely planted copse of small fir trees that acted as a windbreak, and so out on to the open moorland.

The curlews were calling, just as she had known they would. Underfoot, the snow had melted; the bracken was showing green; the heather was springy with the rising sap. Even the Mintlaw burn was bubbling and gurgling with life. She stopped for a moment on a tiny bridge, which was merely a large, flat stone laid across the stream, and dabbled her hands in the clear water. Two sheep trotted up to the stranger and eyed her critically, then decided that she was harmless and bent to their feeding again. There were no lambs as yet in these high places.

It was about eleven o'clock when Annette returned from her ramble. She was tired and hungry, but immensely happy. She had been to the very top of Tod's Knowe, and had picked out all her favourite haunts. Now a gnawing pain inside her told her that she had had no breakfast, and that it would be nice to have a real north-country meal of fried eggs and a slice of home-cured ham. The mere thought of it sent Annette hurrying homewards.

She had got to the high hedge bounding a large field that adjoined the peel-tower on the west, and was just debating whether to scramble through a gap or go round by the gate, when she heard a well-known and hated sound – hounds in full cry. If she had been at home, she would have stuffed cotton-wool in her ears, but, as it was, she couldn't help hearing the uproar. Then she saw a thin russet streak making for the spinney behind the peel. She wished the fox good luck!

Hounds poured over the drystone wall on the far side of the field. Some of the followers were jumping the wall; others were using the hunting wicket on the other side of an old cow-shed. One rider was making straight for the gap in the hedge not far from where Annette stood. The hedge was between them, but she could see that the horseman was a boy. He wore snuff-coloured riding-breeches and a snowy stock, and he was mounted on a big black pony. Annette hated him on sight! He was the hunter, and she was always on the side of the hunted – in this case, the poor fox.

The lone horseman was almost up to the far side of the hedge. In another minute he would jump – smoothly, efficiently. Yes, Annette knew just how beautifully he would jump, hateful boy! A longing to see him make a mess of it shot through Annette's wicked little head. She would teach him . . .! As he gathered his pony for the leap she came suddenly out from behind a hawthorn bush, arms waving, hair flying. The pony swerved, seemed likely to refuse, then changed its mind and crashed through the hedge with a mighty crackling of branches. The boy was off, flung neatly on one shoulder on to a patch of muddy ground at Annette's very feet. She had to admit he had plenty of guts and presence of mind. In a split second he was up and had grabbed his pony's trailing

reins. Then he caught the animal by the bridle and calmed it. After which he turned to Annette, and the anger on his face was such that, for the first time in her life, she felt afraid. She tried to escape through the gap in the hedge, now made appreciably larger by the incident, but the boy caught her by the arm with his free hand and hauled her back.

'Look here – you did that on purpose, did you not?'

As Annette said nothing, he repeated sternly, 'Did you not? You jumped out like that on purpose to unseat me. What did you do it for, I am asking you? Answer me. Do you not know that I might have broken my neck?'

'I wish you had!' cried Annette wildly, though she didn't quite mean that. 'You deserve it!'

'May I ask why?'

'Because you hunt poor foxes,' burst out Annette. 'I think it's cruel! I think it's horrid! I think you're horrible to do it!'

'Oh, you do, do you?'

Still holding Annette by the arm, and his pony's reins in his free hand, he propelled the girl across to the old cow-shed, and before she realised what was happening, he had opened the door, and pushed her inside.

'You shall stay here for a while to think over your sins. I shall come and let you out on my way back,' he said. Then he murmured something more in a language Annette didn't understand, and she heard a slight sound of creaking leather which meant that he had remounted his pony and ridden away.

Annette's French blood rose to her head. She hadn't been hurt, it is true. He hadn't actually done anything to her, but her pride was in the dust. It might have been more accurate to say that it was in the mud, for the floor of the shed was knee-deep in it! Annette Dancy locked in a muddy cow-shed? She felt like screaming; like kicking the door down. She did neither. Her mother's north country ancestry triumphed and told her that it would be stupid to try out such ideas on a cow-shed that was obviously built of the same stout stones as the peel, and whose door was a mighty slab of bog oak, studded with nails. Moreover, there wasn't a single window in it anywhere. Yet a faint chink of light, which made it possible to see at all in the cold, muddy place, must be coming from somewhere. Where was it?

Annette made a tour of inspection, and, in a far corner, almost hidden behind a pile of old sacks, was a long, narrow slit – a loophole window! It was far too narrow for her to climb through. Yet, on second thoughts, she remembered reading that where your head could go, the rest of you could go, too. She decided to try out the theory.

Her head went through easily enough, though one of her ears got a bit squashed in the process, but evidently the book hadn't made any allowance for clothes – not a thick woolly jumper, anyway. Her shoulders stuck in the narrow opening, and there she was, firmly wedged half in, half out. Below her, on the outside, lay a muddy pool covered with clumps of weed. Between the clumps, she could see water-spiders skating about. Below her, on the inside, was a sea of half-soft mud, in which her feet scrabbled about vainly. She had horrible visions of the boy returning and bursting into peals of laughter at her undignified position.

'Not if I can help it!' cried Annette aloud. She remained still for a few moments, gathering up strength. The silence was intense. Then a hunting-horn, thin and reedy, sounded the 'gone away', and she could hear the sounds of the hunt retreating farther and farther into the distance. After that, silence again. The fox had evidently escaped from his hiding-place in the spinney. She was glad of that.

She began to struggle again. She wriggled her head and shoulders round sideways, and finally managed to get them back again into the shed. She felt like sitting down on the floor – if there had been anything to sit on – and howling. It was so infuriating to have to stay there in that dark, cold, muddy place, waiting for that hateful, fox-hunting boy to let her out! She felt as if she were his captive, as indeed she was, shut in his dungeon. Or as if she was a fox waiting to be dug out of her earth. She determined to have another shot at the loophole. Anything better than standing there, doing nothing.

She took off her jumper and skirt and pushed them through the aperture, so that they would be there if, and when, she got out. She wasn't sure whether the boy had merely bolted the door on the outside, or had locked it as well and had pocketed the key, and it would be awful to get out and then have no clothes to wear! Unfortunately, she had forgotten all about

the muddy pool, but she didn't realise that until afterwards.

This time she was more successful. She got her head through easily as before and, by holding her breath, managed to squeeze her shoulders and the rest of her body after them. Thank goodness she hadn't yet had a meal – a couple of fried eggs and a slice or two of ham would have quite undone her! With a last glorious wriggle, she was through – *splash*! – right into the middle of the muddy pool. Water shot up in all directions, but fortunately there were no stones on the bed of the pool – only rushes and a bed of squelchy moss – so Annette had a soft landing!

She picked herself up and looked round for her clothes. Her skirt had fallen clear, but her jumper had landed right in the wettest part. She put on the skirt and was fishing gingerly for the jumper when a slight sound made her turn. Round the end of the shed came the boy, on foot this time.

'Oh, so you have managed to get out,' he said. 'I repented when I had got a couple of fields away, and came back to release you. What are you doing? What is it, anyway?' He pointed to the soggy object in the middle of the pool.

'It's my jumper,' Annette said with dignity. 'I pushed it through the loophole so that I should have something to wear when I got out. I forgot about the water. It's pretty c-cold out here,' she added with a shiver.

'I should say it is!' said the boy. He splashed into the pond in his riding-boots and retrieved the jumper, holding it well away from him. Then he glanced up at the narrow loophole and whistled.

'Fancy you getting through that! Who would have thought it! You are skinny enough, of course, but –'

'I'm *not* skinny!' burst out Annette, as though she hadn't called herself by the name many a time. 'I'm just – just slim.'

'All right – slim, then,' laughed the boy. 'I am not arguing with you. But you are cold, too, by the look of the goose-flesh on your arms. You had better have my coat.' He took it off and held it out.

Annette took a step backwards.

'I wouldn't wear your coat for anything,' she told him. 'It's got blood on it – the blood of the little fox you've just killed.'

'Do not be so hasty,' said the boy. 'I have not killed any fox – not up to date. I have not even seen one, so you can take my coat with a clear conscience, you funny child. Come along, now!'

'I'm not a c-child,' she told him stiffly, trying vainly to stop her teeth from chattering. 'I'm f-fourteen. And you *would* have killed the fox if you'd had the c-chance.'

'Now look,' said the boy. 'I do not suppose you will believe me, but I am not caring the least bit whether I am in at the kill or not. I am really not interested in killing. I am enjoying a day with the hounds, that is all. I would just as soon see the fox go free after he had

47

given us a good run.' He stood holding out the coat.

'I don't want your coat,' repeated Annette. 'I shall wear my own clothes.' She snatched the muddy object out of his arms and began to pull it over her head. The boy snatched it back again.

'You will catch your death of cold.'

'No, I won't!'

'You will!'

They fought for the jumper – like two blackbirds over a worm, as Annette said afterwards. In the end the boy won, or thought he had. He got possession of the jumper, anyway; but, at the same moment, Annette took to her heels and was away over the field, through the gap in the hedge, and had vanished leaving him looking after her in bewilderment.

6 SCHOOL AGAIN

The rest of the weekend sped away as quickly as half-term weekends always do. On the Saturday afternoon the Dancys went to have tea with some friends of their mother. When they got back, Annette was waylaid by Bella, who was holding out what she called a 'fair mucky object'.

'Why, it's my jumper!' exclaimed Annette. 'Where did you get it, Bella?'

'Ye may well ask that, Miss Annette,' said Bella, pursing up her mouth disapprovingly. 'And may I ax what i' the world was your jumper deeing oot i' the field, where yon laddie said he found it?'

'Yon laddie! Which laddie?' But of course Annette knew.

'A bit laddie come to the door and axed to see ye, Miss Annette,' went on Bella. 'And when I said ye was oot, he said to gie ye this.' She handed Annette a bit of paper folded in half and stuck down. 'And how did ye come to get it so wet-like?'

Annette looked up from slitting open the note.

'Ax nee questions,' she said wickedly in broad
Northumbrian, 'and ye'll be telt nee lies.'

'Ye shouldna talk thataway, Miss Annette,' Bella
said reprovingly. 'Whatever would your mam say?'

'She'd say the same hersel', nae doot,' laughed
Annette. 'Mummy can talk Northumbrian as well as
you can, Bella!'

Meanwhile she had opened the note. It read:

Dear Vixen,

*Here is your jumper. I could not dry it, being too far
from home, and I had no paper to wrap it in. I guessed
from the direction you took that you lived in the old peel.
I am sorry I locked you in the cow-shed, because,
although you may not believe me, I am understanding
how you feel about foxes. Also it is good to meet someone
who lives up to their principles! I am sorry, too, that I
thought you were eleven years old, or thereabouts. If I
had known you were the great age you are, I might
have treated you with more respect!*

I am yours with a contrite heart – Angus.

'Eleven?' gasped Annette. 'He thought I was
eleven? The very idea!' However, the letter interested
her. For one thing, it was so very correct. You would
almost think it had been written by a foreigner . . .
And now she came to think about it, the way the
strong boy had spoken was strange, too. He didn't
use a lot of slang expressions as most people did, and
his English was slow and hesitant, almost as if he were

thinking in another language and had to translate. Yet his name – Angus – was English enough. Well, Scottish, anyway. He spoke more perfect English than she did herself, even if he took longer over it. There was something else odd about his way of speaking, but she couldn't quite put her finger on it. She wondered who he was and where he lived. He said he was 'far from home', but that might mean anything. Obviously he was staying with friends, and was, like everyone else, on his half-term holiday.

She was dragged away from her thoughts by Max, who had appeared in the Round Lounge dressed in a pair of black tights, tennis-shoes, and a cricket shirt. He wanted to know what Annette thought of the rhythm he'd made up for his new Spanish number in the forthcoming Ballet Workshop Show.

'Look! It goes like this –' He beat out a series of complicated taps and stamps with his feet, beginning softly, growing to a deafening tattoo, and then dying away again to a mere whisper. At the same time, his fingers beat out a quite different rhythm with the castanets.

'It's wonderful,' said Annette without flattery. She was enough of a Spanish dancer herself to know the difficulty of what he was doing. To the uninitiated it sounded easy – that throbbing, compelling zapateado, but try to do it! Try even tapping out an easy two-four time with your feet, while clicking your fingers in three-four time, and see what a muddle you get into!

Annette was dancing too, now, tossing her head high in a proud, Spanish gesture, tapping with her slender feet, clicking her slim fingers. The strange thing was that when she danced she looked pretty.

'Goodness, what a noise!' exclaimed unemotional Mrs Dancy, appearing in the doorway with a pile of snowy, freshly ironed sheets in her arms. 'Is this for your next show? I think I'll bring along some cotton-wool for my ears!'

'Don't be rude, Mummy!' panted Annette, flinging herself down in a chair. 'Of course it won't sound as loud as that in a big hall. There's only Max doing it, you see. No one else could manage a rhythm like that,' she added with the unconscious conceit of the artiste where his art is concerned.

On the Tuesday morning, by the early bus, Annette and her brother returned to school, and, much more important to them, to their dancing classes. The main object in view was, in Annette's eyes, the approaching Eleanor Brandon Charity Matinée which was to be held in a local theatre, and, in Max's eyes, the Ballet Workshop Show in which he was dancing a jota and a zapateado three nights running. The matinée came first. Oh, the excitement! The triumphs! The awful disappointments! There was nothing else talked about in the dressing-rooms for weeks . . .

'What do you think? Carol's doing the Sugar Plum Fairy! I think it's too bad when she failed that exam.'

'Oh, I know she's good, but she did fail, didn't she, and other people . . .'

'What's that! A Spanish number by Max Dancy! He's hardly what you might call a member of the school, is he, only coming to one class a week? But still, there's no denying it, he *is* spectacular. Anyway, I wish him luck. Tap-dancing yes, but that complicated zapateado – not for me!'

'Has anyone heard about the new ballet, *The Ugly Duckling*?'

'Yes, Marion's the Girl, and Peter's the Boy.'

'Oh, I know that, but who's dancing the main role?'

'Annette Dancy,' said someone over by the door.

A murmur ran round the dressing-room. Then a sharp-faced girl with red hair and cold eyes said nastily, 'Well, I can see Annette Dancy as the Ugly Duckling all right – she's plain enough, goodness knows – but not as the Swan at the end.'

'Well, I don't agree with you, Rachel,' said a girl from the back whose name was Holly. 'Personally, I think Annette will be just perfect for it. And when she's dancing, she's not plain at all. I love watching Annette. Anyway, who else could do it? A dual part like that takes some acting ability – it's *demi-caractère*.'

'There *are* other dancers besides Annette Dancy in this school,' said Rachel.

'Meaning you, I suppose,' said Holly, who disliked Rachel and enjoyed taking her down a peg. 'I expect that's why you *weren't* chosen for the Royal Ballet – too good for them, I suppose?'

'Annette wasn't chosen, either,' retorted Rachel.

'We all knew she hadn't an earthly with that great scratch on her nose, and only one eye. Besides, she's not advanced enough for the Royal Ballet yet. But it doesn't say she won't ever be, or that she isn't good.

Anyway, acting ability counts more than mere technique in a ballet like this.'

'Dear Holly, you know everything,' scoffed Rachel. 'Oh, well, it will be nice to see the mess she makes of it –'

'Shh! Here she comes,' said someone.

They needn't have worried. Annette was walking about in a dream. She had just been told by Miss Brandon that she had got the star role. Yes, Annette Dancy was to be prima ballerina in a real, full-length ballet! No one could have been prouder than Annette was at that moment . . .

And now it was work! During the daytime, Annette existed at school, answering to the best of her ability the games mistress who wanted to know why she wasn't playing hockey. 'I've got a cold, Miss Johnson,' she said with a loud and, she hoped, convincing sniff. As a matter of fact, she had caught a slight cold after her fall in the muddy pool at half-term weekend, but the real reason for her hiding behind the coat-rack in the cloakroom when she ought to have been playing hockey was quite different from the one she had given to the long-suffering Miss Johnson. The real reason was that she was afraid of getting hurt. Past experience made her remember blows on the shins, cracks on the knee, whacks here, there, and everywhere. It wasn't that she minded a broken ankle, mind you, or a torn ligament or two, but the fact that either of these accidents would probably mean the end of her career as a dancer. On small things such as these do the fates of great artistes depend . . .

When Miss Johnson had gone, after ordering the guilty Annette to put on an extra woolly and keep herself warm, Annette sat down on a bench and, taking off her sensible school shoes, stretched out her feet in front of her, and stared at them with interest and, it must be admitted, with admiration. Yes, they were very elegant feet, slim and highly arched. You could see the delicate bone construction underneath the fine skin.

'There's only one thing wrong with them,' said Annette aloud, 'and that's my big toe.' She wriggled the offending toe, which was ornamented with a piece of sticking-plaster covering a blister. 'It's too long for the others. Now if I had four – or even three toes all the same length, how much easier point-work would be. As it is, I have to put all my weight –' the way she said it, you might have thought she weighed at least a ton '– on one toe. No wonder the poor thing gets skinned!'

'Who's that talking in there?' came the voice of Ann, the conscientious prefect.

'Only me,' said Annette meekly. 'I've been excused from hockey by Miss Johnson. I've got a cold.'

'*Someone* was talking – I heard them,' insisted Ann, poking about behind the coats as if, thought Annette, the 'someone' had hung herself up on one of the pegs.

'It was me,' she said again, truthfully, if ungrammatically. 'I was talking to myself.'

Well, everyone knows there are always rules at school about not talking to each other during school hours, but whoever heard of a rule stating 'No scholar must talk to herself'? Poor Ann!

'Well, don't do it again,' she said lamely. 'And if you've got a cold, you oughtn't to be out here.'

'Oh, the bell's just going,' answered Annette hopefully; and, sure enough, just at that moment it went. Annette's cold vanished like snow in summer; on went her hat and coat, *snap* went her case, and she was away down the stairs and out of school. Mere existence had ceased – real life had begun!

7 CHARITY MATINÉE

They say a bad dress-rehearsal always means a good performance. In that case, the Eleanor Brandon Matinée was going to be very good indeed! When Annette panted up the stairs of the Theatre Metropole (back-stage) and made her way to the big dressing-room which she shared with half the rest of the dancing-school, she was met with a chorus of voices: 'My goodness! Hurry up, Annette! Nellie's roaring like a lion! *Everything*'s gone wrong! Half the ballet-dresses haven't come yet, and no one can track down old Gibbs. There's a rumour that she's swallowed a mouthful of pins and been taken to hospital, but I don't expect it's true. Dressmakers just *don't* swallow pins, do they? Otherwise –'

'You talk too much, Carol. But she's quite right, Annette, everyone *is* in a frightful flap, and Carol's tutu hasn't got any frills on the knickers yet, and she can't dance in a tutu with only frills on the top part, can she? It would look as if she'd moulted . . .'

'What a pity she isn't one of the Little Swans, like

Jean!' laughed Annette. 'One can imagine a swan moulting more easily than the Sugar Plum Fairy!'

'It's all very well to joke about it,' said Carol, who hadn't much of a sense of humour at the best of times, and certainly not at a dress-rehearsal, 'but you should just see Maggie. She's turned up with the ballet-dress she wore the year-before-last in the pantomime. It's got pink rosettes all round the hem, and the colour's pale grey. Hasn't been washed since the opening night! You needn't laugh – she's on with me and *I* don't want to be a laughing-stock. What with one thing and another . . .'

'Oh, do be quick, Annette!'

'Now I'm ready,' announced Annette, having pulled up her tights to creaseless perfection, and settled her grey-green tutu.

But, alas, a dress-rehearsal flap was lying in wait for Annette, too! Where was her music – the one and only copy of Chopin's *Préludes*, all cut up, re-shuffled, and marked in red ink by Eleanor Brandon, the choreographer herself – the wonderful music for the new ballet? Like Miss Gibbs, the dressmaker, it had disappeared . . .

'My music! My music!' wailed Annette, rushing round the empty stage in despair. 'Has anyone seen it?' No one had. 'Has someone hidden it for a joke?' No one had. 'Oh, please, please *look*, everyone . . .' Of course it was found in the end – inside the piano, where it had been pushed by a careless passer-by. Of course the elusive Miss Gibbs turned up in the nick of time with an armful of snowy ballet-dresses, finished down to the last hook and eye. Of course Maggie's mother appeared, and promised, word of honour, to wash and do-up her daughter's offending tutu and produce it tomorrow as swan-like as the rest. Of course willing fingers frilled strips of pink net at lightning speed on to the knickers of Carol's tutu, so that the Sugar Plum Fairy should be as beautiful as Sugar Plum Fairies always are. In the end, the last five minutes of the dress-rehearsal went off as well as the first five hours had gone badly. Even Miss Brandon ceased tearing her hair, and vowing that this was the last show she'd ever put on . . .

When at length the crowds of exhausted small girls had been taken home by their even more exhausted mothers, and the bigger ones had stripped off their sticky tights, and mopped their dripping faces with towels – or anything else they could lay their hands on – it might be said that the show was taking shape.

And now for the matinée itself.

It says something for Max Dancy's strength of personality that he charmed that most exacting audience with his Spanish solo. Even more for Annette's, because she was a rival to their daughters. Yet when, in her grey-green tutu, she left the stage, bewildered, beaten by the grown-up swans; when she had been mocked by the cat for not being able to purr, and scoffed at by the hens for not being able to lay eggs; when she had been shot at by huntsmen, and nearly perished with cold; when she crept away to die

they almost felt like weeping. At the end of the ballet, when she appeared, triumphant, they clapped her to the echo.

Annette, bowing this way and that, felt for the first time that thrill that every artiste feels when he, or she, finds she can move an audience to tears. Years afterwards, when she danced on the London stage, she would still remember that wonderful moment.

In the dressing-rooms afterwards, everyone agreed – with the sole exception of Rachel who wouldn't have admitted that Annette was good if she had been Pavlova herself – that Annette had danced well.

'She surprised me,' said Jean to Holly. 'I thought she'd do it well, but not as well as that.'

Miss Brandon, who had seen so many young dancers begin their careers in her big, light studio, merely nodded her head wisely. She had her own thoughts about Annette Dancy, but she kept them to herself. No one knew better than Eleanor Brandon the pitfalls that lie in front of a young dancer; the thighs that become too big, the ankles that weaken, the arches that drop, the stress and the strain . . .

8   THE LETTER

The rest of the spring term flashed by, relieved by the Ballet Workshop Show in which Max took to himself all the honours, and now term was ended, and Easter only a week away. Annette and her brother were at Aunt Molly's flat and were busily packing their belongings for the Easter holidays. Max was throwing things into his case at lightning speed.

'Camera; music-paper; book of Andalusian folk dancing; Life of José Greco; spare pair of castanets; tights; tennis-shoes. That might do me till after Easter.'

'What about a toothbrush and some pyjamas?' suggested Annette.

'Oh, yes,' said Max easily. 'Thanks. I might easily have forgotten them. Can you think of anything else?'

'Lots,' said Annette, 'but by the look of your case, there won't be room! Now, what about me? Let's see – tights, of course. Shan't bother with a tunic. Three pairs of point-shoes. One pair demi-point. Can I borrow your spare castanets, Maxie, then I needn't take any in my case? Thanks . . . Music for *The Ugly Duckling*, so that I can keep it up in the hols – the dance, I mean.'

As they closed their bulging cases, sitting on them to get them shut, the letterbox clattered.

'Post!' said Annette. 'You go and get it, Max.'

Max shot down the stairs to the door.

'It's for you, Annette,' he panted when he returned. 'And it's from Mother. How like a woman to go writing letters the very day we go home!'

'Perhaps it's something special she wants to tell us,' suggested Annette, slitting open the envelope. 'Something so important it can't wait.'

It certainly was!

My darlings, wrote Mrs Dancy, who always included both of them in her letters, though she addressed the envelopes to each in turn.

Before you come home, I have a confession to make! You remember the new vicar and his two children? Well, he is to be instituted next week, and is to 'read himself in' on Easter Sunday. The Squire and Lady Fenwick are putting him up for a week or two at the Hall, as the Lodge isn't ready yet, but they haven't room for the children, when they come home from school, as they have a lot of guests for the point-to-point. So –

'*No!*' cried Annette in such a tone of horror that her brother looked up from the business of tying his case round with string for fear it should burst.

'What's the matter?' he asked.

'*No!*' cried Annette again. 'It's just not possible! It isn't true! It can't be. She says – Mummy says – '

'Spit it out, can't you?' ordered Max. 'What has she done now?'

'She's asked the kids – the new vicar's kids – to – to stay with us for the whole of the Easter holidays!'

'Good lord!' said Max. 'That's a bit tough, isn't it? No wonder she wrote in advance to warn us!'

But it wasn't only the fact of having two strange guests to share their home that had horrified Annette.

It was the rest of Mrs Dancy's letter. She read on: 'It will be nice for you and Max to have Sheena and Angus to share your holiday – Oh, no!' said Annette again.

'Must you keep on saying "Oh, no"?' asked Max. 'It sounds like a worn-out record when it gets stuck and goes on playing the same bit over and over. After all, they may be quite decent kids.'

'But they're *not* kids. That's the point,' said Annette.

'How do you know? Does Mother say?'

'Er – n-no. Not exactly,' faltered Annette, finding it hard to explain. 'But I've an idea they're as old as we are. I've heard that Angus is ever so old.'

'That sounds more like it,' said Max cheerfully. 'It will be a change to have a boy about the place.' He looked at Annette to see what effect his words had. He wasn't above teasing her on occasions. But Annette was far too het-up to rise to the bait.

'You never know,' went on Max. 'I might be able to teach him some Spanish dancing.'

'Oh, no you won't – not Angus!' declared Annette positively.

'You seem to know an awful lot about him,' said Max. 'I thought you didn't even know his name.'

'Shut up!' exclaimed Annette, feeling she was cornered. 'Come on, Max, let's make ourselves some hot chocolate. We've only just time before the bus. If Aunt Molly isn't back before we go, we'd better leave her a note. You know how vague she is. She might easily have forgotten it's end-of-term and wonder where we are. I don't feel like going home now – I feel like staying here.'

'Shut up yourself!' exclaimed Max. 'I think you're making a lot of fuss about nothing, Annette, and that's a fact.'

'You don't know anything about it,' retorted Annette, which was more or less the truth . . .

9 EASTER

Easter was the most beautiful time of the year at home, said Annette to herself, quite forgetting that she thought the same thing at Christmas when glittering frost and snow turned the fir trees in the woods around Dancing Peel into enchanted princesses. It was the same in the height of summer, when the gorse flamed on the moors and the heather came into bloom. And, Oh, how lovely it is! thought Annette, when in the autumn the trees turned colour and the mists hung in blue wreaths in the hollows of wood and moorland. All the same, there was no denying it, spring at Mintlaw took a lot of beating.

The whole village, besides people from the outlying parts of the parish, gathered in the little old church this Easter Sunday morning to hear their new vicar read himself in. The church was beautifully decorated. Round the font were masses of primroses, their little jars of water discreetly hidden by soft green moss gathered from the churchyard wall. The sanctuary was almost hidden by branches of wild cherry blossom, and on the altar white lilies gleamed. They had come out of the Coldburn hothouses. Many tall vases of daffodils stood at the altar-rails, and the pulpit was covered with the lovely yellow blooms.

I wonder if God thinks his house looks nice, thought Annette, who had helped with the decoration the day before. I don't think even Heaven could be lovelier!

She and Max watched the Coldburn pew anxiously to see if the vicar's two children were in it. But no – there was only old Lady Fenwick, who had a face rather like the horse she rode, and Sir William, a kindly old gentleman with silver hair and mild blue eyes.

'I told you, Annette, they don't get here till tonight,' whispered Mrs Dancy. 'And they won't be coming to us until tomorrow, at any rate.'

Annette gave a sigh of relief, which her mother thought was one of impatience.

'Don't worry, dear,' she said soothingly. 'Tomorrow will soon be here.'

'That's the worst of it,' said Annette to herself. 'If only it would never, never come!'

Next day, after lunch, Annette went out to the stables, taking with her a cassette player and a handful of cassettes. She was dressed in an old white tutu that she wore to practise *pas de deux* work at dancing-school. On her feet were an ancient pair of satin point-shoes. Annette pretended that the stables were Covent Garden Opera House. The loose boxes were stage-boxes, and the flat bit of cement that jutted out into the stable-yard was the stage. Many were the happy hours she had spent in the warm, sheltered place, practising her dances at a supposed rehearsal, or dancing the leading role in *Lac Des Cygnes* at an imaginary Gala Performance. Why, she'd even been presented to Her Majesty the Queen at the première of *La Canette Vilaine* (Annette had translated The Ugly Duckling into French because she thought it sounded more professional). In the winter, when it was too cold to dance there, she pretended that Covent Garden was 'closed for redecoration . . .'

On this particular morning she opened the door of the big loose box and going over to a cupboard, pulled out a pile of ballet magazines. In each of them was an *enchaînement*, beginning at the Elementary and going on to the more advanced. Annette sorted them into the right order. Then she put her cassette player on the mounting-block outside the door and put in a cassette. Soon the ancient courtyard was filled with the sound of Chopin's waltzes, and Handel's *Water Music*.

When she had finished the *enchaînements*, Annette had a rest before tackling the Mime Scene from *Swan Lake*. The recording was one that Miss Brandon had made for the school, and had lent to Annette for the holidays. It now sounded very faint and, moreover, extremely tinny. Still, it was unmistakably the Mime

Scene, and in her mind Annette saw the enchanted Swan Princess telling her sad story to her Prince.

She began to dance, and had just got to the part where the Princess explains, in mime, of course: 'If someone me loves' – hand on heart, 'cherishes' – gesture of tenderness, 'marries' – points to ring on finger; when the unmistakable sound of horses' hoofs clattering on the cobbles of the outer courtyard made her freeze to the spot. For a moment she stood motionless, arms outspread in a lovely flying gesture, for she was just telling her Prince of her enchantment.

Then she dashed to the cassette player and switched it off, just in time to hear a voice exclaim, 'What an awful noise!'

Annette knew that slow, measured voice. There was no mistaking it! She stood there, waiting.

Round the corner of the outer courtyard, into the inner one where she stood, came two figures. Yes, there was no mistaking the foremost. He was leading a pony, the same big black pony he had ridden the day she had unseated him in the field. He wore a kilt and a rough tweed jacket, patched with leather at elbows and pockets. Grudgingly Annette had to admit he looked striking. Tall and well-built, just the figure to wear the kilt. Behind him, mounted on a chestnut pony, came a girl. She was obviously younger than he was, fourteen or fifteen, Annette thought. She had red-gold hair, slanting green eyes, and a small red mouth showing little white pointed teeth. She made Annette think of a cat. Not a nice, fat, tabby cat, but an aristocratic pedigree cat, spiteful and cruel. Her chestnut pony's coat shone like her own auburn hair.

The boy stopped short when he saw Annette; partly from surprise, for she certainly must have looked unusual, to say the least, standing there in her tutu, pretending to be an enchanted swan!

'Oh, I am sorry,' he said at length. 'I did not mean you to hear what I said.'

'I didn't mean you to hear my music, either,' said Annette coldly.

'It wasn't that I didn't like it – the music, I mean,' explained the boy. 'I am very fond of music, Tchaikovsky in particular. That was why I could not bear hearing it murdered like that. I apologise, though.'

'I suppose you are one of the Dancys?' broke in the strange girl in just the sort of soft, throaty voice Annette had known she would have. 'The one called Annette.' She laughed. 'Annette Dancy – what a funny name!'

'Talking of names,' said the boy quickly, 'my name is Angus Alexander MacCrimmon, kin to the Mac-Crimmons of Glendale in the Island of Skye. My father's grandfather was hereditary piper to the Mac-Cleod of MacCleod. He – my great-grandfather – was a descendant of Black Lad, who was the grandest piper of them all. His music was given to him by the fairies. When his lord died in battle, it is said that Black Lad took himself away into a wild and lonely corrie in the Black Cuillin, and there in the mist and the rain played his lament for his chief.'

Annette looked at him in astonishment to see if he was joking. But no, he was obviously as proud as a peacock of his descent from a great-great-grandfather who was piper to a Highland chief somewhere in the Island of Skye!

All right! thought Annette, I'll show him!

'*My* father,' she said, 'was Edmond François Dancy, and *his* great-great-great-grandfather was Count Alphonse Ludovic d'Ancy of France, a great favourite at the Court of Queen Marie-Antoinette. *My* family came to England during the French Revolution – to escape the guillotine,' she added grandly.

'Oh!' said the girl, obviously a little taken aback, as well she might be.

'Yes, and that explains what you call my "funny name",' said Annette. 'By the way, what's yours?'

'Sheena Macdonald,' said the other, 'of the Macdonalds of Glendounie in the Island of Skye, who are kin to the Macdonalds of Sleat, who were one-time Lords of the Isles. I am not Angus's sister, as everyone here seems to think. I am his cousin. In the Gaelic my name is spelled S-I-N-E, but I use the English spelling. People find it easier.'

'That sounds just as funny to me,' declared Annette.

'Look,' broke in Angus, as though he felt the atmosphere growing tense, 'can we put our ponies in one of these places?' He nodded towards the loose boxes.

'No, I need them for my dancing,' said Annette.

'But my dear good child, you can't need all of them,' said the boy, reasonably enough as even Annette in her calmer moments had to admit. After all, you couldn't expect the sort of boy he was to understand about Covent Garden, could you? 'How about this one? Both the animals could go in there, and there's a hay-rack. There isn't one in any of the others. You certainly don't need a hay-rack for your dance practice, do you?' He made clicking noises through his teeth at his pony and led him forward.

'No, no, you can't go in there!' exclaimed Annette, barring the way. 'That's the Royal –' She stopped herself just in time. How he would laugh if she had told him this one was the Royal Box!

'All right, one of the others, then. Which one?' He stood waiting.

'I know you've come to stay with us,' burst out Annette. 'I know I've got to be polite to you because you're a visitor, but you'll please take your horrible horses somewhere else. This is my stable, and these are my horse-boxes – all of them!'

A flicker of anger passed over the boy's face.

'Now look,' he said, 'you've got it a little wrong, haven't you? My father made it quite clear, when he agreed to live in the Lodge, that we would need the use of the stables. My father rides, you know. In fact we all do, and there is only one small stable down at the Lodge. So you will please clear your stuff out of two of these loose boxes, whichever ones you like, by this evening. If you have not done so by then, I shall do it myself.'

He swung himself into the saddle, and turned to ride out of the stable-yard.

'Stop!' cried Annette. 'You can have your loose boxes. You can have them all! I don't want to stay here now.' With dignity she gathered up her magazines and thrust them back into the cupboard, picked up the cassette player, and stalked out with it.

They were over, the long, peaceful days when she was able to practise her dancing unseen and unheard. No more would the quiet stable echo to the tap-tap of point-shoes or to the faint, unearthly strains of *Swan Lake*. The floor of the Royal Box would be covered with straw. Instead of a symphony orchestra there would be hissing noises made by Angus Alexander MacCrimmon as he groomed his pony, and the low scoffing laugh of his cousin, Sheena, as she sat on an upturned bucket and cleaned her tack. The picture Annette conjured up was too much for her. She burst into tears and fled.

10 THE KITTEN

It's difficult to go on hating a person when you're living in the same house with him, especially if that person does everything possible to make friends with you, and has lovely manners into the bargain. When he stands aside politely to let you pass on the stairs, and looks after you at mealtimes. Yes, very difficult, thought Annette. Also, it was a fact – everyone else seemed to like Angus; even Max, her temperamental brother.

'Quite a decent chap that Angus,' he said one morning, about a week after the arrival of the visitors. 'Got quite a good idea of music.'

'From his great-grandfather the piper, I suppose!' said Annette sarcastically.

'You needn't laugh at him,' exclaimed Max. 'I expect to be a piper to a Highland chief is no end of an honour – even leaving out the bit about the fairies.'

'What's that about fairies?' asked Mrs Dancy, coming in to clear the breakfast table.

'We were just talking about Angus's great-grandfather,' explained Max. 'He was descended from a piper called Black Lad who was given his gift of music by the fairies. Angus says so, anyway, and I really think he believes it.'

'I expect he does!' laughed Mrs Dancy. 'The Mac-Cleods of Dunvegan Castle have a flag that was given to them by the fairies, and woe betide anyone who laughs! When one goes to Skye, one even believes in the 'wee folk'. Angus is such a nice boy, isn't he? Where is he now, by the way?'

'Oh, he's gone to the stable to groom Black Bess, his pony,' said Max. 'And Sheena's there, too. Her pony's name is Morag.'

Annette thought, Even Mummy has fallen under Angus's spell! Aloud she said, 'I'll help you to wash up, shall I, Mummy? Then Bella can get on with other things.'

'Thanks, Annette dear, if you would,' said Mrs Dancy. 'And really I must be thinking about lunch. Five of us, not counting Bella. It's quite a big family!'

'What about Sheena?' said Annette. 'Can't she help, too?'

'Well, she's a visitor, darling,' said Mrs Dancy, though she couldn't help thinking, like Annette, that the Scottish girl might have offered to lend a hand. 'You can't ask visitors to help if they don't offer. Angus is going to ride into Bellingham after lunch and do all my shopping. I do think it's nice of him.'

After she had helped with the washing-up, and made her bed, and set the table for lunch, Annette went out into the village to see all her friends, of whom she had a great number.

Now, although Annette had a quick temper, was imperious to a fault, and was often anything but reasonable, she had her virtues, too. She stuck to her principles through thick and thin – not only when it suited her, but often when it didn't. She did nothing by halves. So when she got to Postie's Cottage, where old Sally Muirhead lived, and heard the sad story of poor Timmy's leg, she fairly boiled over with rage.

Timmy was old Sally's cat, not a tomcat but several times a mother – the name had been an accident! Just a few days ago, Timmy had proudly presented her mistress with one more litter of kittens. There were three of them. They were a rusty brown colour, with black smudges in all the wrong places, but Timmy thought they were beautiful and she spent all her time washing and feeding them. Old Sally loved them, too, ugly though they were. She vowed she would find homes for them all when they were big enough.

And then, as she told Annette, the awful thing happened. Timmy had gone out, and hadn't come back. All day long Sally had looked for her. All day long her saucer had stood, brimming with milk, beside the basket in which squirmed the three forsaken kittens. The tiny creatures began to nuzzle each other, trying to find their mother, for they were, of course, still quite blind. They were also, as might be expected, extremely hungry by this time. Their pathetic cries nearly drove poor old Sally to distraction.

She tried to feed the tiny creatures with spoonfuls of milk, but they were far too young.

'Oh, Miss Annette, it fair drove me oot o' ma mind, it did that, to see them puir bit kitlings!' she told her visitor. 'And then I found her. She was in old Johnny Makepeace's field, doon by the side o' the wood, and fast by the leg in a trap. One o' them beastly gins, it was! The puir beast had hung there on the bankside arl neet lang, and it sae wet and cald. Well nigh froze to death, she was! A couldna get the puir thing oot the trap as a didna know how to open it, so a pulled it up and carried it, kitcat and arl, hame to ma cottage.'

'Then what did you do?' said Annette.

'Well, as luck would ha't, Jimmy MacKlintock, the veterinary, happed to be at the Keenlesides, doctorin' ane o' their coos, so off I runs and gets him. A nice, canny man is Jimmy MacKlintock. He taks puir Timmy oot the trap, and awa' wi' her in his car to his surgery at Bellingham, and he cuts off her puir leg, for it was mangled beyond repair, says he, and 'twas the only way to save her life. But she'll recover, says he. Cats ha' nine lives, and this nobbut Timmy's fifth or sixth.'

'Oh, poor Timmy!' said Annette tenderly, as she looked down at the cat lying so still in the blanket-lined box that Sally had rigged up for her.

'She's still dazy-like,' explained Sally.

'But the kittens?' said Annette. 'What about the kittens?'

'They're deed – arl except ane,' said old Sally, tears

coming into her eyes. 'The puir wee things! They might ha lived if she'd been able to feed 'em yesterday, but she was far too ill, puir creature. She canna even feed the wee one that's left, and it only just alive.'

'Oh, Sally, how awful!' exclaimed Annette in horror. 'But we can't – we *can't* let it die, just like that. There must be something we can do. Let me have it, Sally. Give it to me, I'll feed it somehow. I'll manage, you'll see.'

'Little and often, the veterinary said,' explained old Sally, as Annette took the kitten and wrapped it up tenderly in a bit of old blanket. It was no longer a fat, prosperous kitten, but a poor, thin, cold creature, about as big as a large-sized mouse. 'I'm afeared it's done for, but ye canna dee nae harm. The veterinary said that, supposin' we could keep it alive wi' glucose and milk for a day or two, Timmy would mebbie tak it back and feed it hersel' – when she recovers a bit like.'

'I'll do it, you'll see,' vowed Annette. 'You'll see, Sally.'

She hurried home with the tiny creature.

'Mummy! Bella! Max!' she called. 'Oh, come and see what I've got!'

They all came running, Max in his tights, and Bella wiping her hands on her apron. Mrs Dancy's hands were all floury from the pie she was making for lunch. Angus and Sheena, dressed in their riding-clothes, came running, too, to see what all the noise was about. Everybody talked at once:

'Where did you find it, Annette?'

'Oh, Annette, the poor little kitten. Run for some milk, somebody, it's only just alive . . .'

'Oh, the puir wee thing,' came Bella's deep, rumbling Northumbrian voice, acting as a sort of bass accompaniment to the rest.

'Och! The ugly wee kitten,' said Sheena with a shudder. 'Take it away, it makes me feel sick.'

Only Angus said nothing. Annette was to learn, as time went on, that Angus always said less than other

people, and did more. He took the tiny creature gently from Annette and tried to coax it to drink. He succeeded in getting a drop or two into its little pink mouth, but most of it ran out at the sides again. All the time he talked to it in a strange, soft language that none of them understood.

'It is the Gaelic,' he explained apologetically, seeing their questioning faces. 'When I am sad, or very angry, I am saying it in my mother-tongue.'

All day long they tried to feed the kitten. Although they didn't seem to be very successful, they must have persuaded it to drink a little milk, because by the evening it was still alive, though very weak. Angus had gone off to Bellingham on his pony to do Mrs Dancy's shopping, as he had promised, and had not yet returned.

'Surely it can't have taken him all this time,' said Mrs Dancy anxiously, when ten o'clock came and there was still no sign of him. 'Besides, the shops will have shut long ago . . . Oh, there's the telephone! Answer it, will you please, Annette. It will be Mrs Whitehead about the Women's Institute Concert on Friday. She said she would ring up –'

But it wasn't Mrs Whitehead. It was Angus, to say that he would be late back, and please not to wait up for him.

Poor Mrs Dancy looked more worried than ever.

'It's all right,' said Sheena, looking up from the book she was reading. 'You need not worry about Angus. He is used to going about by himself. In Skye he was often gone for days, climbing, and so on.'

'Y-es I suppose he is old enough to look after himself,' said Mrs Dancy. 'Still, in a strange place . . .'

'Oh, but it isn't strange,' Sheena assured her. 'We have often come here and stayed with the Macdonalds of The Braes. That was partly why he wished to come here, I think.'

'Well, I told him where to find the key,' put in Annette, 'and he said it would be all right, so I think we ought to go to bed, don't you?'

It was midnight by her little bedside clock when Annette woke up. At first she couldn't think what it was she had to do. Then she remembered – the kitten! She must feed it. She tiptoed across the room quietly, because she was sharing it with Sheena, and opened the door. On her way along the cold, stone passage, she passed Angus's room. The door was ajar, and she peeped inside. There was a full moon, and she could see by its light that the counterpane on the bed was unruffled, and that the bed itself hadn't been slept in. So Angus hadn't returned yet!

Annette went carefully down the spiral staircase to the kitchen and opened the door. A draught of warm air met her.

Then Annette realised that somebody was standing over by the window, and before she could cry out, a voice said, 'Shh! Don't waken the house!'

Max! thought Annette. I might have known he'd remember the kitten!

The figure moved to switch on the light and with a shock Annette saw that it wasn't her brother, after all.

'Angus!' she exclaimed. 'Whatever are you doing here in the middle of the night?'

'I might ask the same of you!' he answered. 'What are *you* doing, walking about in the cold without any slippers on?' His tone was teasing, but Annette chose to call it bossy.

'Well, someone had to get up to feed the kitten,' she retorted.

'Which is what I am doing,' said Angus. He took something out of his pocket as he spoke, and Annette saw that it was a small feeding-bottle. She watched him light the gas stove and pour a little drop of milk into a saucepan, adding glucose. This he heated until the chill had been taken off. Then he poured it into the feeding-bottle. After this he put it to his own lips to see if it was drawing properly.

'Good,' he said after a moment. 'Now watch!' He kneeled down beside the kitten's basket and Annette saw him gently put the teat into the little creature's mouth.

'Oh!' said Annette. And then, 'Oh!' again. She could hardly believe her eyes. The milk was disappearing out of the bottle, and the kitten was swelling visibly as they watched it.

'Its own mother couldn't do it better!' said Angus triumphantly.

'But when did you get it, and what made you think of it?' demanded Annette.

'I have often fed a lamb out of a feeding-bottle,' said the boy, 'so it struck me that the same thing ought to apply to a kitten, only the difficulty was to get something small enough. I tried in Bellingham, but of course they had nothing, so then I thought of a toyshop. The nearest place was Newcastle, so I went there by bus. There wasn't a bus back to Bellingham, but I managed to get a Carlisle one along the Military Road, which brought me as far as a place called

Chollerford. Then I got a lift from a man in a car as far as Wark and walked back to Bellingham, where I had left Bess. After that, it was an easy ride. It took longer than I imagined it would, though, so that was why I rang up – in case your mother thought I had got lost or something.'

'She was a bit worried,' said Annette.

'I am sorry about that,' said Angus. 'Indeed, there was no need for her to be anxious. This is not at all wild country like my home in Skye.'

Well, thought Annette, as she watched Angus feed the kitten and slip a hot water bottle into its basket, it just shows that it's all a matter of comparison. Most people regarded Dancing Peel and the village of Mintlaw, and indeed Northumberland generally, as the back of beyond. The wildest, loneliest place imaginable. Yet here was Angus obviously thinking about it as if it were Piccadilly Circus!

11   THE FEUD

In a couple of days you wouldn't have known that kitten! So fat had it become, thanks to the feeding-bottle, that, as Annette said, it had at last begun to look like a real cat instead of an undersized rat.

'This cat is quite disgusting – all tum!' commented Max.

'It isn't disgusting at all,' exclaimed Annette. 'I think it's just beautiful! I shall call him – I mean her – Sheba. I shall take Sheba back to her mother after breakfast.'

'I hope you've hit on the right sex this time,' observed Max. 'Don't forget it was you, Annette, who named poor Sheba's mother Timmy!'

They all – except Sheena, who turned her back upon the kitten in disgust, saying that it now reminded her of an overfed mouse – went in triumph to Sally's cottage with their precious charge. Timmy, though still weak and ill and a shadow of her former beautiful self, took her offspring back with loud purrs of affection. Even with only three legs she could still wash it.

It wasn't until they were back at the peel that Annette remembered hastily that Angus was her enemy. She was reminded of it during the morning, however. Mrs Dancy and Bella were having their eleven o'clock cup of coffee, and Annette was ironing her ballet-dress in readiness for the Women's Institute Concert at which she was dancing that evening, when in strode Angus. Annette saw in a moment that he was off to the meet. No one would get dressed up in such immaculate breeches, such a snowy stock, and gloves which had obviously been newly washed, for just an ordinary ride! She had been feeling friendly towards Angus since the kitten incident. Now her heart hardened against him.

'Hello, everybody!' he said. 'Do you think I could have a cup of coffee, too, Mrs Dancy? I shall not be in to lunch – Oh, thank you, Bella! No, I do not take sugar . . . What is it that you are doing there, Annette?'

He sounded surprised, and no wonder! Annette was almost hidden behind masses and masses of white net – the four full-length skirts of her *Sylphides* ballet-dress, each one of which had to be ironed separately.

'I should think you could see. I'm ironing,' said Annette, so shortly that her mother looked at her in astonishment.

'Annette is dancing at the concert this evening,' she explained, seeing that Annette obviously wasn't going to offer any explanation herself. 'There's a play, you know, by the members of the WI, and we're all helping. I'm helping with the supper, and Max is giving us a Spanish number. He's working the curtains, too. Not that they need much working really,' she added, 'you just walk along with them at the end of the scene!'

'You needn't let Angus know how primitive we are, Mummy!' exclaimed Annette.

'Och, you need not worry about that,' laughed Angus. 'In Skye when we had anything of this sort, we were not troubling to have curtains at all!'

'I suppose your great-grandfather played at all the local dances,' said Annette, trying to think of the most insulting thing to say.

'Och, yes,' said Angus, not seeming at all insulted. 'At least he would have, if he had been there. Grandad was always ready to oblige with an eight-some reel, or a foursome, but of course he lived away in Glendale, which is a very long way from Portree where we lived, so I did not see much of him – except when I went to stay there.'

Annette didn't answer. She had come to the end of the last skirt, and, lifting the dress carefully, she carried it away. Angus politely opened the kitchen door for her and when she came out of her bedroom, she found him waiting for her.

'Annette –'

'I'm in rather a hurry.'

'Yes, so am I, but I must speak to you, Annette.'

'Well, be quick then,' said Annette, 'though I can't imagine what you want to say.'

'You are still angry with me about – about what happened the day we met?'

Annette said nothing.

'Can we not be friends? I am wanting so much to be friends with you, Annette.'

'No, we can't be friends,' said Annette. 'Not while you hunt foxes.'

'Can you not live and let live?' said Angus, choosing an unfortunate expression, it must be admitted. No wonder Annette blazed at him.

'Live and let live! Do you think of that when you go hunting?' she burst out.

'You are knowing what I mean. I do not question the things you do, however foolish I might possibly think them.'

'*So!*' exclaimed Annette, her French blood rising. 'You think I am foolish?'

'I did not say so. I said that I might possibly think some of the things you do are foolish, and if so –'

'You needn't go any further,' said Annette. 'I *quite* understand. You think I am foolish! You think my dancing is foolish! You think –'

'I think what I said before – that you are a vixen!' said Angus, losing his temper.

'How dare you call me a vixen!'

'I shall call you what I please! We are enemies, are we not? Then look out for yourself! To be at enmity

with a MacCrimmon of Glendale in the Island of Skye, a descendant of Black Lad –'

'Oh, don't be silly!' said Annette, getting in the last word, as she had a little habit of doing. Now that she had flown at him, her anger had evaporated somewhat and she felt a little uneasy. She didn't want to be friends with him, of course, but she didn't want to be – well, exactly his enemy. Still, she'd said what she had, and she was too proud to go back on it. Also, she reminded herself firmly, he did hunt. There was no getting away from that fact. Meanwhile, he was still standing there with that stern, proud look on his face.

'I must go,' said Annette. 'I've told you; I'm in a hurry.' Since he was standing between her and the door, she ducked under his arm and fled.

12   THE CONCERT

Every year the Mintlaw Women's Institute gave a concert, at which the chief item was a play. This year there were to be several other items of interest and, last but by no means least, Annette Dancy in dances from *Les Sylphides* and her brother Max in *Danse Espagnole*.

The village was in a fever of excitement. For one thing, the new vicar was to be there. It was the first time some of his parishioners had seen him. It was the first time they had seen Annette and her brother dance, too. And besides all this, the play, *A Moss-Trooper's Bride*, was said to be the best the Women's Institute had ever done. 'A reel knock-doon thriller!' pronounced Martha Keenleside, and she ought to know for she was to play the male lead, namely the dashing moss-trooper, a Border raider, himself!

It's well known that accidents will happen at amateur theatricals, and the Mintlaw Concert was no exception to the rule. It was bad enough when Willie

Muirhead got confused with the lighting arrangements and, instead of putting the spotlight on Max, plunged the stage into total darkness right in the middle of the most dramatic part of *Danse Espagnole*. It was even worse when the feckless Willie fell over the record player and broke it, so that all the special music that was to create 'atmosphere' for *A Moss-Trooper's Bride* was lost to the waiting audience. It was sheer catastrophe when the leading lady – or perhaps that should be gentleman – fell full length down the improvised staircase at the back of the stage and sprained her ankle.

'Oh!' moaned Hangman Hal, which was the name the moss-trooper went by. 'Oh, me leg! It's broke! What's to dee noo? What aboot the play? A'll no can dee it!'

And, indeed, no one looking at the poor woman's ankle, already swollen to the size of a cricket-ball and getting bigger and blacker every minute, could doubt the truth of her words. She certainly couldn't do it!

'Well, what about her understudy?' demanded Max, putting his head round the screen that did duty for a dressing-room. 'You'd better tell her – the understudy – she's to go on in Martha's place.'

The members of the Women's Institute looked at each other and muttered in dismay. Understudy. There was no understudy. Hadn't they had a hard enough job in the first place to get anyone to learn the part of Hangman Hal, let alone getting someone to learn it without much chance of performing it? No, understudies weren't popular in Mintlaw. People want a part or nothing at all. Without Martha, the show just couldn't go on . . .

'Can't it?' a voice from the other side of the screen said. 'How about me?'

The members of the Women's Institute stopped twittering. They were struck dumb with surprise. Here was Max Dancy offering to take on the principal role – just like that!

'B-but you haven't learned the part,' objected the producer, a large lady with greying hair and horn-rimmed glasses.

'Oh, haven't I?' Here Max appeared wholly from behind the screens, a strange figure dressed in tights, shirt, and most of his Spanish make-up. 'That's all *you* know! You forget I was at the last two rehearsals – working the curtains.'

'Yes – but two rehearsals – the chief part –' the producer faltered, remembering how long it had taken Martha to learn her lines.

'I've got a very good memory,' Max assured her. 'Really I have. Ask Annette! I can say every word of it. Listen!' He began to reel off the dramatic utterances of Hangman Hal.

'Well?' said Max. 'Will I do? It's me or nothing, remember, and if I forget a few bits here and there I can easily improvise, you know. Had a lot of experience in the plays at school.'

'He's right,' said Annette, coming out of the ladies' dressing-room in her petticoat and point-shoes. 'He's first-rate. I say it, though he is my brother. You let him do it, Miss Winterburn.'

'Well, all right then,' agreed that lady in desperation. 'Let the play go on!' After all, as Max said, it was that or nothing, and her reputation was at stake. For many months past she had laboured on this play, and now to have triumph snatched from her by a sprained ankle! 'On your shoulders, Maximilian,' she added dramatically, 'rests a great – a very great responsibility.'

'Okay,' said Max cheerfully, not seeming unduly crushed in spirit by the thought. 'Give me five minutes to get into the clothes. Tell you what – play 'em some music, somebody.'

Meanwhile, behind the scenes, all was feverish activity. Poor Martha had been helped into the ladies' cloakroom and her ankle had been bandaged. Max had disappeared behind his screens once more, and when he reappeared there was a gasp of admiration from all sides. The exotic Spaniard had given place to a no less exotic Hangman Hal. He was tall and slim, with elegant legs and a purposeful swagger, partly due to the fact that Annette had pinned the spare material of his coat into two large pleats at the back. His eyes glittered, owing to the Spanish make-up which he hadn't had time to remove. His voice, low and menacing, could be heard right to the further-most corner of the hall.

The village was thrilled. Never had they seen a play with such a fascinating villain. At first they didn't know who the actor was. Then the news ran round the hall like wildfire.

'Aye, it's young Maximilian Dancy. Who'd ha' believed it! A' thought he was naught but a school-boy!' Even Miss Middlemas, the village school-mistress, who played the heroine, the Lady Lucinda de Lacy, was thrilled to the marrow by her leading man.

'Come, my Lucinda, my fair one,' said Hangman Hall with bloodcurdling menace in his tones. 'Your lily-livered lover is far distant –'

'But it is you, Hal, you that I – that I –' Miss

Middlemas was so fascinated by the spectacle of Hangman Hal advancing upon her, coat tails swinging, eyes glittering, that she forgot her words. In a panic she backed away from him towards an antique fireplace that formed the back of the stage.

'Adore!' hissed the prompter from the wings. '*Adore!*'

'Adore,' repeated Lucinda faintly, still backing.

'Keep away from there!' ordered Max in his ordinary voice. 'You'll have it over!' Then in stage tones: 'If thou wilt not come willingly, my pretty one, then I shall take thee by force!' Max had also forgotten his lines and was improvising shamelessly. He lunged forward and swept his pretty one into his arms, only just in time to save her from being engulfed by the antique fireplace, which chose this moment to fall flat upon the stage, exposing a large wooden clothes-horse, a large box with TINNED LUNCHEON MEAT – PRODUCT OF NEW ZEALAND stamped on its side, and another with BAKED BEANS IN TOMATO SAUCE on its middle in large black letters.

'Ow!' yelled Miss Middlemas. 'Put me down, Maximilian, you naughty boy!'

'Hangman Hal, thou meanest, my cooing dove,' corrected Max, enjoying every minute of it. 'Oh, all right, only why you can't enter into the spirit of the thing . . .'

'You weren't meant to do that,' Miss Middlemas told him indignantly, settling her crinoline. 'You were meant to offer me your arm.'

'Dear lady,' said Max, with a low bow, 'you would have been beneath yon fireplace, had I not acted quickly. Anyway,' he added in his own voice, 'much more dramatic the other way. Listen to that! You see – they liked it!' The village audience was fairly raising the roof with applause, stamps, whistles, and catcalls.

'We'll have to appear before the curtain,' announced Max. 'Come on!' Before poor Miss Middlemas had time to protest he had swept her up in his arms again, and marched on to the stage with her to the huge delight of all the schoolchildren who had never thought to see their schoolmistress in such a position!

'Oh, Max! You were naughty!' giggled Annette, trying vainly to see herself in the small mirror that was hung on the back of one of the screens, and settling the wreath of white flowers she wore with her *Sylphides* dress. 'Poor Miss Middlemas! It wasn't meant to be like that at all and you know it!'

'It was too tame, if you ask me,' said Max. 'I brightened it up a lot! Useful being a dancer. You know how to pick people up, and she's no mean weight, is our Miss Middlemas, although she looks so skinny.'

'Shh, she'll hear you,' warned Annette. 'D'you mind if I borrow your make-up mirror? This one is so tiny I can only see one eye at a time . . . Oh, thanks! I'm on next – will you work the cassette player for me, Max, please? You know where the dance starts.' She hummed a snatch of the waltz, and her brother nodded. 'Wish me luck . . .' By the expression on her face, you would have thought that Annette Dancy was going to perform before royalty, at least, instead of to a village audience. But it was always like this with her, she put her whole heart into her performance, no matter how small or how uncritical her audience might be.

Unfortunately the villagers – the male population, anyway – didn't appreciate classical ballet. They preferred tap-dancing, Scottish dancing, something with a bit of 'go' in it. They began to make rude noises and titter.

Poor Annette faltered and wavered in a lovely arabesque. She was temperamental, like all true artistes. Her mood broke. Why, why, she thought in agony, did I choose this particular dance? I might have known they wouldn't understand it . . . it's all wrong for here . . . it's a village hall filled with hooligans! I can't dance here . . .

All these thoughts flashed through her mind during that arabesque. And then, suddenly, the rude noises ceased. The mood of the audience changed. Annette felt it immediately, as those who perform on the stage always do. Her own former mood returned. They liked her dance, after all! She leaped across the stage in a grand jeté, landing as silently and as gently as a leaf falling. Her arms were as pliant and as graceful as the branches of a budding willow tree in spring. Some people might call them skinny; some people might call Annette herself skinny; but Angus MacCrimmon, standing at the back of the hall, thought she was beautiful. The intense love of music that was in his blood, inherited, no doubt, from his ancestors, made him thrill to her every movement. She might be his enemy; she might be a little vixen, but she was also the most graceful, the most enchanting girl he had ever seen. Evidently his father thought so, too, because when Annette retired behind the screens, after bowing times without number to a now wholly enslaved audience, she found Mr MacCrimmon waiting to congratulate her.

'Your mother told me you learned ballet,' he said, 'but I had no idea you could dance like that. May I congratulate you, my dear!'

Annette looked up at him – he was very tall, very like Angus. In spite of his being Angus's father, she couldn't help liking him.

The surprise of the evening, to Annette at any rate, came in a few words from Miss Winterburn, the producer. She had come into the dressing-room to congratulate Annette, for she was a keen lover of ballet.

'That was lovely, Annette,' she said. 'I've never seen the Waltz done more beautifully. Of course I've seen it done better technically, but never with more feeling. What a blessing that boy Angus came to the rescue in the nick of time, wasn't it?'

'Angus? What has Angus got to do with it?' demanded Annette, pausing with one leg out of her dress. 'I didn't know he was here, anyway.

What do you mean, Miss Winterburn?'

'What, don't you know what happened?' said Miss Winterburn. 'Didn't you hear those awful boys – Andy Carter and Robbie MacFarlane – making the most dreadful noises?'

'Y-yes, I heard some noises at the back,' faltered Annette.

'They are really bad boys,' went on Miss Winterburn. 'What they came to the concert at all for, I can't imagine. But Angus MacCrimmon dealt with them as they deserved, turning them out like that!'

'What?' exclaimed Annette. 'You mean he –'

'Yes, he took them by their coat collars, one in each hand, and put them outside. Then he leaned against the door and refused to open it. Not that anyone wanted him to, mind you. Those lads were just making themselves a nuisance, only no one else would have dared to do it. But if it hadn't been for him . . .'

Yes, thought Annette. If it hadn't been for Angus, my dance would have been spoilt! Then she sighed. Oh, if only Angus wasn't the sort of boy he is, how nice he would be!

That night they were all in high spirits. Mr MacCrimmon came back to supper and proved to be great fun. They played charades, at which the young Dancys were experts, and finished up with murder in the dark all over the ancient peel-tower, after which they were almost too frightened to go to bed!

Annette couldn't help noticing how young and

pretty her mother looked. Mrs Dancy was wearing a new dress of a lovely soft shade of green. She had made it herself, and it went well with her fair hair. It wasn't often, thought Annette with a stab of conscience, that her mother had anything new. Usually it was her or Max. Then she noticed that her mother was looking tired, too.

'Oh, Mummy,' she said, when Mr MacCrimmon had left and Max was locking up. 'Mummy – what did you sigh for? Was it because you're tired, or because I snapped at you yesterday? I know I snapped – I didn't mean to, but I did.'

'Annette, you funny child!' said Mrs Dancy. 'No, of course it was nothing to do with you. I don't even remember your snapping, as you call it. As a matter of fact I sighed because a statement of Daddy's royalties came today, and I'm afraid it was very small indeed – £5.75 in fact! Not much good for your dancing lessons, Annette, or for school fees. No wonder I sighed. Oh well – thank goodness this is a good time of the year for the poultry.'

Annette flung her arms round her mother's neck in an agony of remorse.

'I'm sorry I snapped, Mummy,' she sobbed. 'I won't again, I promise.' With one last hug, she rushed away upstairs and flung herself down on her bed.

Poor Mrs Dancy. She felt like sighing again. It was always the same, and always would be, she feared. Annette danced in public with such grace and

perfection, but after it was over she felt the strain, and all her family felt it too. Sometimes Mrs Dancy wondered if she ought to let her go on with it. But then, she thought, you couldn't stop her. It was in Annette's blood, just as it was in the blood of her lovable, temperamental Max.

Upstairs, Annette was crying her heart out, and when Annette cried she did it properly. No stifled sobs for her, they were more like banshee howls! Angus, going to the bathroom, couldn't help hearing. He stopped outside her door.

'Annette,' he said softly. 'What is the matter? May I come in?'

Receiving no answer he went in, and stood looking down at the forlorn figure on the bed. It was hard to recognise in her the radiant dancer of a few hours before. No wonder Angus was puzzled.

'What is the matter, Annette?' Fortunately, he thought, there was no one else in the room. Sheena had gone over to Coldburn and was staying there the night. He couldn't imagine what Sheena would have thought of it all.

'I snapped at Mummy,' sobbed Annette, 'and she looked so tired; and I snapped at you, too, Angus, and then you s-saved my d-dance for me.'

'Saved your dance? I do not understand you. What is it that you are meaning?'

Then, between sobs, his ears caught names – Andy, Robbie . . .

'Oh, you are meaning those lads I turned out of the hall while you were dancing. I think it was time someone did it. I was glad to be of use to you, Annette.'

'But I snapped at you,' insisted Annette, determined to be a martyr.

'I am taking your word for that,' said Angus, 'although I do not remember. However it is quite probable, I must say! You see – I am beginning to know you, Annette. I am sure you were not meaning any harm. Shall we let bygones be bygones and be friends? What do you say?'

'I would like to be friends with you, but I can't,' hiccoughed Annette.

'Why not?'

'Because you follow the hounds. I've already told you.' Then she added with something of her old spirit, 'I can't be friends with anyone who hunts foxes, but I'm sure your great-grandfather was ever such a nice old man, and I'm sorry I snapped at you, and thank you for what you did at the concert. Now, please go away.'

'You are a funny wee lassie,' said Angus. 'Well, let us have a truce, shall we, between you and me?'

Annette nodded.

'Yes, we could do that if you like, only please go away. I'm so tired.'

'I am just going,' said Angus. 'Good night, Annette.' He shut the door and went on his way with a very puzzled expression on his face.

As for Annette, she dried her tears, remembered an *enchaînement* Miss Brandon had taught the class on the last day of term, worked it out carefully, and did it faultlessly round the room. After this she undressed, got into bed, and dropped into a dreamless sleep – much more dreamless than that of anybody else in the peel, Max, perhaps, excepted . . .

Part Two: Summer

1   THE SUMMER TERM

Annette hated the summer term. She hated the long, hot days in school, working out impossible problems in arithmetic and algebra. Annette was very bored.

Outside, the pavements shimmered in the heat, and a haze hung over the industrial city. Even the Eleanor Brandon School of Dancing was feeling the heat, and opened its windows wide, so that strains of *Swan Lake* and Handel's *Water Music* met you half-way up Rothbury Crescent. An interested crowd of small children and a few grown-ups stood every night at the street corner, looking up at the windows, and shouting epithets, rude and otherwise, whenever a dancing figure came into view. Sometimes all they could see was a forest of arms waving in graceful gestures; sometimes they were luckier and beheld dancer after dancer whirling past the windows of the big studio.

'Coo!' one small onlooker would exclaim in an awestruck whisper. 'That takes some doing, I bet! Our Jill's in there,' nodding towards the windows.

'She's practising for the panto auditions. She's good, is our Jill. That's her, see.' A tiny waving figure of a child at the nearest window proclaimed that this was 'our Jill'.

Sometimes, on a hot, thundery evening, Annette wished she could skip a class and go off swimming with her schoolmates, or have a game of tennis after the sun had gone down, or perhaps spin out of town for a breather on a bicycle. But she never did. She was practising far too hard for her Elementary exam, and one class a day was none too many. Besides, she wasn't supposed to swim or play tennis for fear of overdeveloping her muscles.

Yes, thought Annette, mopping her streaming face with a towel after a particularly hard class on a particularly warm evening, you had to give up an awful lot of things you'd like to do when you decided to be a ballet-dancer. But her determination never wavered. Most children of fourteen haven't the least idea what they want to do or become when they leave school, but here, in Miss Brandon's classes, were a few who did. Every so often a pupil would turn from a plump baby to a skinny ten-year-old, to a slender ballet student diligently practising at the barre, with legs and arms seemingly made of rubber.

Annette Dancy had all the requisites which go to make a classical ballerina, and when you have heard them, you will wonder that any one girl has them all! Perfection of body; not too tall, too short in the neck, too big in the hips, too thick in the thigh. An expressive face; mere prettiness doesn't matter. Musicality; or how could she dance with the music? A well-educated mind; or how could she interpret her roles? A clever brain; or how could she follow the intricate *enchaînements* thrown at her by examiners, teachers, and ballet masters, many of them foreign? Besides this, our ballerina must possess the constitution of an ox to be able to stand meals at all sorts of odd hours and odd places, or to go without them altogether; to be able to stand class after exhausting class, rehearsals, fittings, photographings, and then to appear on stage as if she had just risen from her couch. But every dancer accepts all this without question, and indeed wouldn't have it otherwise.

The only relaxation Annette enjoyed was an occasional week-end when she and her brother caught the bus to Whinsheil, the nearest village to Mintlaw, and walked home in the long summer twilight over the four miles or so of moorland to their home. It never seemed to grow dark at Mintlaw during those long June days. Up on the moors it was cool and scented. The lambs had been born and had grown fat, and were now nearly as big as their mothers. Timmy's kitten was already prowling in the dyke bottoms, looking for fieldmice, with Timmy hopping along a little way behind on her three legs.

Every week, Mrs Dancy wrote to her children and told them all the news.

My darlings, she wrote.
Only a fortnight to the end of term! I know how you will both be longing for a sight and smell of the country, after the heat and smoke of Newcastle!

Nothing very exciting has happened here since you were over three weeks ago. We had the Rothley WI to an Open Night last week, and a Mrs Handiside came up to me and said she'd heard all about the splendid play we had put on at Easter, but of course it was no wonder it was good, seeing that we had a film star in it! So you see how Max's fame has spread!

Mr MacCrimmon is getting on well in his new

parish – all the people seem to like him, except old Mary Jane Judspeth, who says he's 'ower tall' and she can't look at him without getting a crick in her neck! I hardly think we can blame poor Mr MacCrimmon for that, can we?

The repairs to the Lodge are going ahead at a great rate. I forget what stage they were at when you were over here, but now the roof is on, and they have made the front window (the one looking over the little bit of lawn) into a french one, so that you can walk straight out of the living-room into the garden, without having to go right round by the door. The old washhouse at the back has been made into a nice bathroom, and they are going to enlarge the woodshed and make it into a stable for the vicar's hunter. It seems unnecessary, really, when we have all those empty ones up here, but he insisted. Angus will still keep Black Bess in our stables when he is at home. There wouldn't be room for her in the new stable. Angus has left her up at Coldburn while he's away. They have a groom who will look after her.

At the present moment, Mr MacCrimmon is staying here with us as Sir William and Lady Fenwick are in London for a week, visiting their daughter. He has been spending his evenings fixing up a new hen-house for the chickens (the March hatched ones), which are getting quite big now and need a house to themselves. He sends his love to you both. The Lodge will be finished in a week or ten days, so by the time you and Max are home for the holidays, he and Angus will be settled in

*their new home. Sheena will be spending most of her
holidays there, too.*

Much love from Mummy.

*P.S. Angus will be coming home from school the same
day as you. It will be nice to see him again – I have
missed him quite a lot. I think he is a delightful boy.
The vicar laughed when I told him how sure we were
that the new vicar's child would be a horribly spoilt little
boy. That hardly describes Angus, does it?*

Max, who had been reading the letter over
Annette's shoulder, burst out laughing.

'It certainly doesn't! Why, you could hardly say
he's little now, and as for being spoilt – well, Angus's
worst enemy couldn't call him that.'

The whole-hearted admiration in her brother's
voice sent an unaccustomed stab of jealousy through
Annette's heart.

'Don't breathe down my neck, Max,' she ordered.
Then she added quite unreasonably, because only a
moment ago she'd been thinking very kindly of
Angus herself, 'Well, *I* think Angus is very spoilt.
What about our stable?' She had, of course, told her
brother all about that affair.

'Well, I must say I think he was right there,'
declared Max. 'What did you want with three loose
boxes all to yourself, anyway?'

'But you know very well it was the Royal Box he'd
asked for,' Annette said, shocked. Surely, surely,

116

Max, an artiste himself, would understand. But apparently Max didn't.

'I think you were being a bit uppish in that particular instance,' he said. 'I thought so at the time, only you were so cross I didn't like to say so. Couldn't you have let the chap have the Staff Box, or the other one, without yelling "You can have them all!" and flouncing off the way you did?'

'Because I couldn't *live* my roles with him leading his beastly pony in and out!' flashed Annette. 'And anyway, how do you know I flounced out? You weren't there.'

'Knowing you, I can guess!' said Max with a grin.

'It's all very well for you,' said Annette. 'You've got your den. How would you like it if Angus sat down in your den when you wanted to practise your zapateado?'

'Okay by me!' said Max. 'Nothing would please me better. It's grand to have a man about the place, instead of a lot of dithering girls –'

'Meaning me, I suppose!' broke in Annette. 'Right! You can get a *man* to do your Spanish *pas de deux*, then, instead of a dithering girl!'

'Now do have a spot of common sense,' said Max, seeing that he had gone too far. 'How can a man be my partner in a sevillanus?'

'I haven't the least idea,' said Annette haughtily. 'That is for you to find out.' So saying, she began to practise déboulés all round Aunt Molly's dining-room table. She had worn quite a track on the carpet by this time which, fortunately, Aunt Molly was too short-sighted to notice . . .

'Stop a minute,' begged Max, dashing round after her. 'Annette! I didn't mean that you were a dithering girl. Honestly I didn't! Stop doing those things for a minute and let me explain.'

'You needn't trouble,' said Annette, finishing off the déboullés with a dramatic treble pirouette. 'Anyway, I haven't time to bother with your sevillanus tonight. I have too much *real* work to do.'

With this parting shot, she snatched up point-shoes and tights and departed, leaving Max to follow in her tempestuous wake later on.

Girls! thought Max. There's nothing so unreasonable as girls!

2 SUMMER AT DANCING PEEL

Neither of the Dancy children could ride, the chief reason for this being that there had never been enough money to spare for ponies, not even one between them. As far as Annette was concerned, there was another reason too, but she kept that to herself.

It was on a Tuesday morning, at the beginning of the second week of the holidays, that Annette, looking out of her bedroom window, beheld an astonishing sight – her brother Max astride a rakish chestnut pony, charging across the heather 'as if', she said afterwards to her mother, 'the foul fiend was after him!' He wasn't dressed for riding, either. He wore black tights and ballet shoes, and he was yelling '*Olé*! *Olé*!' at the top of his voice.

'Maxie! Maxie! Whatever are you doing?' shouted Annette from her window.

Max looked round as best he could in the circumstances and, seeing his sister leaning out of her window, tried to pull up the pony. But Rufus, the pony, had other ideas! Away he shot towards the doorway leading into the walled courtyard where, judging by urgent whinnies, another pony awaited him. And away with him went Max, clinging to his mane for dear life.

'I – learning – to – ride!' came Max's voice on the wings of the wind. 'Sorry – can't – stop.'

After a few minutes, back he came, still on the pony, and following behind came another pony, a big black one with a tall, fair boy in the saddle.

'I am teaching Max to ride,' announced Angus.

'Yes – I'm – loving – every – minute – of – it!' shouted Max breathlessly.

'I am loving it, too,' said the precise voice of the Scot. 'Would you like to learn to ride, Annette?'

'No! No, no, no!' cried Annette.

'Why not?' asked Angus, pulling up his pony below the window where the girl was. 'Are you afraid?'

'Afraid? No, of course not!'

But it was true – she was afraid. She was so much afraid that at the mere sight of a horse something turned over in her inside and she felt sick with fear. Her thoughts flew back over the years to her eighth birthday, when a village lad named George Sowerby, meaning to be kind, had picked up the tiny creature that was Annette Dancy in those far off days and set her on his pony 'for a birthday treat'. The pony was frisky, and feeling nothing on his back instead of the accustomed weight of George, bolted headlong,

jumping the Mintlaw Burn that crossed his path and lay between him and his stable. The tiny girl on his back was flung headlong, landing in the middle of the burn.

The frightened George had rushed to her rescue, and indeed, if he hadn't been very quick, she would surely have been drowned, for she lay there in the water, all the breath knocked out of her.

'Dinna tell no one, Annette,' the frightened boy had begged. 'Me dad'll flay us alive if he was to get to know.'

'But it wasn't your fault,' Annette had said with chattering teeth.

'All the same, dinna tell. Dinna tell.'

'All right, I won't,' promised Annette, and being a lady of her word – even at eight years – she hadn't. Not even Mrs Dancy knew why her daughter was such a coward when it came to horses.

'I just don't like riding. I don't like horses,' Annette told Angus from her window.

'What? And you a Northumbrian!' he teased. 'Come awa doon, Annette Dancy, and I'll let ye ride ma ane wee Black Bess.'

Angus, Annette had already discovered, was intensely proud of his Scottish descent, and often spoke in the broadest of Scots, and also in the Gaelic, although at other times he spoke the purest English, and only his slightly stilted phrasing betrayed him for the Highlander that he was.

'No, thank you,' she said, politely but firmly.

'Och, it's all right,' said Angus. 'I only thought to ask ye. Your brother is doing fine.'

But Annette had already disappeared. In a few moments the two boys, looking up, beheld her on the flat roof doing her barre work. The low stone coping, which acted as a rampart, made an excellent barre – just the right height.

It was to the roof that Angus came after he had finished giving Max his riding lesson. He stood still for quite a long time, watching the graceful, dancing figure of the girl. Then he came forward.

'Annette –'

'Well?' Annette said regally. She had just finished the Sugar Plum Fairy's solo, and she was feeling her princely rank. 'What do you want?'

'I want you to come back to your stable,' said Angus seriously, having no notion that his words, to an outsider at any rate, sounded at all strange.

'My stable? Oh, you mean to dance there?' said Annette, fixing her dark, luminous eyes upon him. 'No, thank you.'

'Oh, please,' begged the boy. 'I want you to.'

'Why?' Annette asked bluntly.

'Because I like to see you dance,' confessed Angus. 'I'll keep Bess up at Coldburn, in the stables there, if you like. It's only a mile and a half to walk.'

If Annette had been older for her age, or if she hadn't been so 'one-way minded' as Max put it, she would have been touched at the sight of the boy's utter capitulation, at the idea of his walking a mile and a half each day for his pony, and a mile and a half back again at the day's end, just for the sake of one small, black-haired girl who had charmed his artistic Celtic soul with her grace. But Annette thought only of her art.

'I'm quite all right here,' she declared. 'It's too much bother to move now.'

'Oh, please,' begged Angus again. 'I hate to think that I turned you out. I'll move your things –' he made a movement towards her cassette player and tapes.

Annette waved him back with an imperious gesture that might have done credit to Prince Siegfried in *Swan Lake*.

'I am quite all right here,' she said again in her most grown-up manner. 'I was a little annoyed at the time, but now I think I actually prefer it here – I'm less likely to be disturbed. In the winter, I may change my mind.'

There was nothing for Angus to do but go back to his pony and ride away across the moorland, where the grouse rose at his passing, and the craggy peak on the far horizon reminded him of the mountains of his island home.

It's the blue islands are pullin' me away, he thought, feeling suddenly homesick in his unhappiness. I'd give anything to climb old Alasdair, and see the sun set over Rum and Canna . . .

3   THE BIRTHDAY PARTY

Annette had eight weeks' holiday from school, but only two weeks' holiday from dancing. Every day, except on Mondays and Saturdays when there was a bus from Mintlaw, she walked to Whinsheil and caught the bus from there into Newcastle. She had two classes a day now, one in the morning and one in the afternoon. Sometimes she even had a third after tea. The all-important Elementary exam was at the end of September, just before school began, so that was why all this work had to be done during the holidays. Once, when she climbed wearily down from the bus and set off on her three-mile walk home, she met Angus riding along on an ancient bicycle that he had borrowed from Tommy Robson, the black-smith's son. Angus seemed to have made quite a lot of friends in the village already.

'Hello, Annette!' he hailed her. 'Tired?'

'Yes, a bit,' she admitted. 'It was a very hard class.'

'Hop on the step of my bike and I'll give you a lift,' said Angus.

They sped along the narrow, white moorland road, and were home in no time. After that, it was amazing how often Angus happened to be in Whinshiel, 'doing a bit of shopping' at the general store, about the same time that Annette descended with stiff and aching limbs from the Newcastle bus.

And now it was the beginning of September, and tomorrow was Angus's birthday – his sixteenth.

'What are you going to do to celebrate?' asked Annette. It was Friday, so she was feeling delightfully lazy with the weekend in view, although, as a matter of fact, there did happen to be a class tomorrow, and a very special one at that. 'What a pity there isn't any hunting in the summertime! Never mind, there will soon be the cub-hunting!' She had grown quite fond of Angus, but she wasn't above giving him a sly dig now and then.

'I can do very well without hunting,' declared Angus. 'Especially at this time of the year. I shall have a picnic and I shall invite you both.'

'A picnic? Oh, where?'

'On the very top of Peel Fell,' announced Angus, 'where there will be a beautiful breath of fresh air.'

'You've said it!' exclaimed Max. 'A hurricane, most likely. Why Peel Fell? There's not much on top of Peel Fell but a rock or two, a peat-hag, and a lot of rushes.'

'You have forgotten the view,' said Angus quietly. 'It is magnificent. You can see the Carter, and Cheviot, and on a clear day you can see the sea. In the other direction, you can see right over into Scotland.'

'You seem to know more about this place than we do ourselves,' remarked Annette, 'though we've lived here all our lives.'

'You get to know the countryside when you ride over it on horseback,' he answered. 'Besides, I am no stranger to these parts. I have often stayed with the Macdonalds.'

'Oh, yes, Sheena told us that,' said Annette, getting up and perching herself on the rampart. 'I suppose you came for the hunting.'

'Yes, the hunting,' agreed Angus. 'That was before I knew you, Annette.'

'Well, I'm not sure that I can come to your party,' she told him. 'I have a class tomorrow.'

Angus's face fell.

'Oh, but it is Saturday, and I am thinking –'

'I know it is, and I don't usually have classes on Saturday. Elaine Ritchey is coming from London tomorrow to give a free RAD class, so I can't possibly miss it, even if I wanted to.'

'Meaning you do *not* want to?' said Angus, quietly.

'I never want to miss a ballet class,' declared Annette.

'Then you do not want to come to my picnic?'

'Annette, dear,' said Mrs Dancy, who had joined them on the roof, 'couldn't you go to the picnic *after* the class? After all, if it's in the morning – the class, I mean –'

'I'll think about it,' said Annette.

'You could get a bus out from town to Falstone, and another one to Deadwater,' said Max. 'We could meet you –'

'Yes, we could do that all right,' said Angus eagerly. 'We could ride over there in the morning. It would be good practise for Max. Then we could ride to the top of the Fell, or anyhow, part of the way up, to have lunch, and then ride down again to meet your bus – either at Deadwater or Plashetts, wherever we find it stops. After that we could all climb to the top, unless I could persuade you to ride Bess.'

'No,' said Annette with a shudder. 'What about you, Mummy? Are you coming, too?'

'Oh, yes, Mrs Dancy – of course you are included in the invitation,' Angus said.

'Thank you very much, Angus,' laughed Mrs Dancy, 'but I'm afraid I can't accept, much as I'd like to. You see, the WI are doing the jam and the fruit-bottling tomorrow, over in the school. It's for the Market Stall. There are all the jars and the bottles to carry over – they've been stored here in the peel. Your father has offered to help.'

'Then that only leaves Sheena,' said Angus.

But Sheena said she didn't feel like having tea on the top of a stupid little hill like Peel Fell. She would rather stay at home.

When Annette arrived at her ballet school the next morning she found the big studio crowded with disgruntled dancers. The girls were standing about in their best tights, freshly ironed tunics, and brand-new hairbands, the boys in snowy shirts, their hair neatly plastered down on their heads.

'What's the matter?' demanded Annette. 'You all look frightfully glum.'

'So will you,' said Carol, 'when you hear the shattering news. The free class is off! It's been postponed until Monday.'

'Oh, no!' wailed Annette. 'I came in specially.'

'Hard luck!' said Joe, one of the boys. 'Can't be helped, though.'

'Why couldn't someone have let me know,' grumbled Annette, flopping down on the floor and leaning her pointed chin on her knees.

'Couldn't, darling,' answered Cynthia. 'Only knew ourselves five minutes ago.'

'But what happened?' asked Annette. 'Why can't she come?'

Everyone began to talk at once:

'I wouldn't care, but it happened last time.'

'She went over her time at her Leeds class and missed the train, so that was why . . .'

'Doesn't think the provinces worth the bother . . .'

'If you ask me, she's absent-mindedly forgotten about us and gone dashing back to London.'

'Rubbish! She wouldn't do such a thing, not Elaine Ritchey . . .'

'Oh, wouldn't she? Bet she would!'

'Bet she wouldn't! She's one of the most decent of them.'

'I wasn't saying she wasn't decent; I was saying she was absent-minded . . .'

'Oh, be *quiet*, everybody,' ordered Annette, 'and let me think!'

It says something for her personality that there was a sudden hush in the studio.

'Think away, darling,' said Carol. 'Thinking won't do anyone any harm, though really I don't see what there is to think about. We may just as well all go home.'

'What? And waste a whole morning's practice!' exclaimed Julia, who was taking the Elementary exam with Annette and was very serious about it. 'Perhaps it's a good thing Miss Ritchey hasn't turned up. Think what a lot of barre work we can get done.'

'Barre work's all very well,' grumbled Annette, 'but we can do barre work any old time. It's tips we want; a lesson from someone who will put a little extra polish on our dancing and give us a few new angles. Oh, well – as long as she really does come on Monday, I suppose it will do. Come on, everybody, barre work it is!'

She marshalled them on to the barres without more ado. Although she was by far the smallest in the class, though not the youngest, she took command. Annette might lack height but she had force of character to spare! The studio rang with her curt commands, and anyone listening outside the door might have thought it was Miss Brandon herself taking the class.

'Oh, well,' she said at length, loosening her dark

hair out of its net. 'I think that's enough. I can get an earlier bus home, if I go without my lunch.'

'You'll faint by the wayside,' said Cynthia, a round-faced student who had definite ideas about lunches – and other meals too! Cynthia had no illusions about herself. She knew she had neither the face nor the figure ever to succeed on the stage, so she was fully resigned to her career as dancing-mistress.

'Oh no, I shan't,' answered Annette. 'I shall eat my sandwiches in the bus. Anyway, I shall make up for it at teatime. I'm having a picnic tea on top of Peel Fell. It's someone I know's birthday.'

Her fellow students looked at each other significantly. They had given up trying to understand Annette Dancy. She was 'just Annette' and that was that!

'Well, goodbye, darling,' said Cynthia, rubbing some cream into her freckly nose. 'Hope you get there – to the top of wherever it is!'

'Goodbye,' answered Annette, cramming her dancing kit back into her case. 'I hope so, too.' Then she added, 'I suppose I shall have to wash my tights again and iron my tunic, and tomorrow's Sunday. Bother! Why can't dancers behave like reasonable people?'

She never asked herself whether she, as a dancer, acted as a reasonable person. Whether, in fact, she was doing so now, catching a bus before the one she had said she would catch. It never occurred to her, as she got out at the tiny village of Deadwater, that when she determined to climb Peel Fell by herself, she might miss Angus coming down.

I'll be there before he's started, she thought with a chuckle. It isn't very far. How surprised they'll both be to see me here so soon!

It was a perfect September day, with a hot sun, but a faint nip in the air that made you think of brambles in the hedgerows, and gossamer spiders' webs enmeshing the tall bracken fronds along the dykes. It had been hot and stuffy in the bus, and Annette stopped at one of the new cottages that had just been built by the Forestry Commission and asked for a drink of water. She also asked if she might leave her case until she returned. The fresh-faced country-woman gave her a glass of milk, and watched her curiously as she climbed the drystone wall out on to the moor proper. People always noticed Annette. Partly it was the way she moved, and partly her grown-up manner, combined with her extremely youthful appearance. You couldn't treat Annette as a child. She wasn't a child in the ordinary sense. She knew exactly what she wanted to do in life, and she intended to do it, by hook or by crook.

Up the steep hillside she went, and the sun beat down upon her. Straight in front was one of the young fir woods which were now clothing the bare, round hills of the Cheviot country with a living mantle of green. Cutting right through it was a fire-break. It looked, thought Annette, as if it would be a wonderful short cut to the top of the mountain, whose summit you could just see through a gap in the trees. You could walk up that beautiful, mossy, green lane, with the tall trees on either side, and you'd be there in no time at all. Much easier than the rough, grassy moorland over which she was now walking. She looked at her wristwatch. It was only two o'clock. She had a whole hour before Angus would start on his way down to meet her.

She made for the fire-break, squeezing under a couple of fences and crossing a small field of rough grass to reach it. Oddly enough, it wasn't nearly as smooth as it had looked from down below. In fact, as

Annette progressed, it became very rough indeed. Mossy green lane was quite the wrong description – jungle was more like it! Giant clumps of willowherb and rushes, waving white banners, barred her path. Nettles and thistles rose up along the edges of the wood, higher than her head. There was heather, too, in great, round, purple cushions and, of course, the inevitable bracken, wearing its flaming bronze mantle of autumn.

'The strange thing is,' she said aloud, 'I can't see the top of this lane, and, whereas before I thought it was quite straight, now I'm not so sure – Oh! What happens now?' In front of her the track divided in a perfect V, and, over the top, exactly in the middle, rose the illusive top of Peel Fell. It seemed farther away than ever. 'Which one do I follow?'

The right side was rather less rough so she chose that and plodded on doggedly. Flies followed her in a dense, black cloud, and every time she stopped, they stopped too, and settled on her.

'Ugh!' said Annette, clapping her hands. 'This is awful! Shoo!' The cloud rose, only to settle again when she stopped clapping.

She dashed into the fir wood to the right in an effort to get rid of them. The ruse succeeded so long as she stayed in the dim and scented depths, but when she emerged, back came the flies in their thousands.

The going became worse and worse. Across the path lay channels in whose dark depths trickled sluggish, brown, peaty water, and Annette had to be very

careful indeed where she put her feet – her precious, dancing feet! If she stumbled into one of these treacherous places and sprained her ankle, her ballet career might be ended . . .

'Why, oh why, did I ever come to this horrid place?' she said aloud. 'I must go back – even if I *am* late.'

She retraced her steps for what seemed miles, and the odd thing was, that although she ought to have been going down, the lane seemed now to be going up. Moreover, suddenly it turned a corner that certainly hadn't been there before, and here, in front of

her, was another confusing V. Somehow, somewhere, she had gone astray, perhaps when she had
plunged into the wood to rid herself of the flies, and
she was now lost. Lost in the Kielder Forest!

'I can't be lost!' she cried aloud. 'If I keep on going
up, I must come to somewhere!' But the trouble was
that the lane would seem to be going up, and then
suddenly down it went again. It was horribly confusing, and horribly, terrifyingly tiring.

Annette was a country child. She was used to
moors and lonely places. She wouldn't have minded
being lost out in the open moorland, or even in a
wood – an ordinary wood, that is. But this dense,
dark place wasn't like an ordinary wood. It went on
for ever, seemingly. She felt shut in, as if the trees
were pressing down on her, intent upon smothering
her.

The afternoon wore away and still Annette plodded on. She had danced all the morning, between
long bus journeys, and now she had walked for many
miles in this jungle of nettles and willowherb, tor-
mented by flies, burned by the sun, her feet sore and
blistered by the rough ground. A more miserable
creature than Annette Dancy it would have been hard
to find!

It grew dusk, with still no sign of the forest's
ending, and it grew cold. Annette crept into the
undergrowth at the edge of the wood and lay down
on a bank of fir needles. It made quite a comfortable
bed, and if only she hadn't been so cold she might

have gone to sleep. As it was, she lay awake listening fearfully to the faint noises that make a country night anything but quiet – rustlings and scuttlings, hootings and squeakings. Once something cold nosed against her face, and she leaped up with a shriek of terror. It was only a hedgehog, but Annette's imagination ran riot. Who knew what strange things dwelt in the depths of the Kielder Forest? It might even have been a wildcat! She had seen one once on the lonely moors round Kielder, standing on a crag. Wildcats were the most fierce of animals, more savage than leopards . . . So ran Annette's thoughts as she dragged her weary limbs onwards, only to fall once more, utterly exhausted, on another cushion of fir needles.

She must have slept at last, because suddenly the moon was high in the sky and beside it twinkled one lone, frosty star. She sat up, wondering for a moment where she was, then remembered. She was lost in the Kielder Forest! She might wander for days and nights, and be found at last, dead of hunger and exhaustion, by a woodman – if she wasn't eaten by a wildcat first . . .

Then suddenly her hair rose on her head. Something black was moving in the darkness, coming up the fire-break towards her. Something neighed. Tales of the dread water-horses of Skye told her by Angus flashed through Annette's head. She sprang up and fled for her life into the jungle behind her, crashing through the branches, not even feeling the nettles that whipped her face as she forced her way through them.

The black shape divided into two shapes, and one of them dashed after her.

'Annette! Annette!' said a voice, a human voice – surely not that of a water-horse! 'Don't be

frightened! Don't run away! It is I – Angus. Where are you, Annette?'

'Oh, Angus, why didn't you say so before!' exclaimed Annette, stopping in her tracks, and waiting for him to come up to her. 'Why didn't you come and find me before? I've been frightened to death!'

Angus was silent for a moment. The sheer unreasonableness of this speech left him without words.

'But how was I to know where you were?'

'You might have guessed,' said Annette, brightening up now that the danger was past. 'I caught an earlier bus, and took a short cut, only it didn't turn out to be a short cut.'

'I think I am doing very well to find you at all,' declared the boy. 'From half past three I am scouring the countryside. If that woman at the cottage had not seen you climb the wall and come this way, I should never have found you. I should never have thought of looking for you in this place, never!' Now that his anxiety was over, his anger flamed. 'Do you know,' he added sternly, 'that there are search parties out looking for you? Men, tired after a long day's work, have had to turn out and comb the moors and the woods, just because one stupid –'

'Be quiet!' ordered Annette in something of her old regal manner.

'I shall not be quiet, and you shall listen to me,' said Angus. He switched on his torch, and the sight of her scratched and nettled and swollen face melted his heart. He couldn't even go on being angry with her.

139

After all, it was just Annette, and she couldn't help herself. 'Come along, now. I have got Bess here. She is back in the lane –' he nodded over his shoulder '– if she has not taken herself off. You can ride her.'

'No,' said Annette with a shudder. 'No, thank you, I won't ride.'

'You will do as you are told,' said Angus. 'I am knowing that you dislike horses, but it will not hurt you to sit on Bess for a short while. I shall walk alongside.'

'No,' repeated Annette.

'Yes!' insisted Angus firmly.

When they got back to the lane they found Black Bess still there, nibbling the grass. All day long she'd been ridden hard, and she was ready for a rest and a meal.

'Up you go!' said Angus. He lifted the girl into the saddle, taking no notice of her protests.

'I t-think you're d-dreadfully unkind,' hiccoughed Annette. 'You know how much I h-hate r-riding.'

'I daresay Bess has not exactly liked scouring the countryside all the day long, and half the night, looking for one small girl who has no more sense than a – than a –' Angus sought about for the right word '– a wood-louse. Personally I think you ought to be grateful to her for not turfing you off.'

Annette didn't answer. For one thing, she had remembered about the free class on Monday and her precious feet. They had taken terrible punishment already, and it was up to her to save them all she could

– even if it meant riding a detested horse. Besides, it wasn't as bad as she'd thought, riding Bess. Not with Angus walking alongside. She couldn't help relaxing as she swayed in the saddle. Her poor, aching feet began to feel more comfortable.

'When we get out of here on to the short grass I can ride behind you,' said Angus, breaking in upon her thoughts. 'Ah, here we are.' The wood had suddenly come to an end. Below, not more than a mile away, lights twinkled. The village of Deadwater.

'Then I haven't been so far away from home, after all,' said Annette, astonished.

'No – you were probably never more than a couple of miles,' said Angus. 'Most of the time I expect you were walking along parallel to the edge of the wood. I shall show you on the map sometime.'

'But how did you know where you were?' asked Annette.

'I am looking it up on the map first, and I had a compass,' Angus told her.

He swung himself up behind her, and on they went. Annette's head fell against his shoulder. He put his free arm round her to steady her.

It's quite nice riding on Bess, ran Annette's thoughts. Quite nice . . . She sighed with relief. Safe, too, with Angus here . . . so sleepy . . . ever so sleepy . . .

'Wake up, Annette! I do believe you have been asleep,' came a voice, rousing her.

'Asleep? Of course I haven't.'

'All right, I am taking your word for that. You must dismount now, though. We must see what has happened to the search-parties and poor Max – he will be quite frantic. Also your mother –'

'Oh, poor Mummy!' exclaimed Annette, realising at last the anxiety she had caused. 'We must ring her up straight away. And I've just remembered, Angus – it's your birthday, and I haven't wished you many happy returns of the day.'

Angus laughed. 'That is all right, Annette. I do not know that I am wanting to live today all over again!'

'But I've got a present for you,' insisted Annette, rummaging in her pocket. 'Look – it's a hankie with your initial on.'

He took the handkerchief from her.

'Thank you – thank you very much, Annette,' he said gravely, folding it, and putting it carefully into his own pocket. 'I shall keep it always.'

'Oh, it's not a terribly good one, I'm afraid,' said Annette off-handedly. 'You see, I had to do the initial myself because it was cheaper, and it's not very well done. Needlework isn't my strong point.'

Angus smiled at her old-fashioned manner.

'I am liking it so much better when you are working it yourself,' he said in the soft Highland accent he always fell into when he was moved by emotion, be it pleasure or anger. 'I am thanking you, Annette, for your birthday present.'

'Oh, that's all right, Angus,' Annette told him. 'It was a pleasure.'

4   SHEENA

It was quite by accident that Annette found out that Sheena could dance. Not ballet proper, of course, but still, there was no doubt about it, the Scottish girl had quicksilver in her heels. . . .

It happened like this. Mrs Dancy had taken the new vicar and his family under her motherly wing, and now, when it was a question of a new winter coat for Sheena, she at once offered to take the girl to New-castle and get it for her.

'If we make it Tuesday, we can all go in together,' she said. 'Annette can go off to her dancing-class, while Sheena and I choose the coat.'

It was clear from the first five minutes in the shop that it was Sheena who was going to do the choosing, and not poor Mrs Dancy.

'It must be green,' said the girl. 'Green is my colour.' She ran her eyes over the garments on the stands, and pointed to a coat. 'That is the one.'

It was probably quite by accident that the coat she chose happened to be the most expensive one on the rail. To be fair to Sheena, she didn't appear even to look at the price on the label. Also, it was true, the coat was obviously made for her. Its lines flattered her slender, graceful figure; the misty green colour matched her eyes and brought out the tawny lights of her auburn hair.

'It's a little expensive, dear,' said Mrs Dancy. 'Your uncle . . . your mother –'

'Oh, Uncle Malcolm won't mind,' replied the girl. 'It has nothing to do with him, in any case. And, as for my mother,' she shrugged her shoulders, 'I have my own allowance, you know.'

Mrs Dancy didn't know, but it was no business of hers, and she said no more.

After the coat had been paid for, Sheena having produced her own cheque book, the two of them had coffee in the restaurant, and then Mrs Dancy proposed that they go to Rothbury Crescent to call for Annette.

'We can have our lunch in the park,' said Mrs Dancy. 'I've got a flask of coffee in my shopping bag, and I saw that Annette brought plenty of sandwiches in her case.'

'Oh, but Mrs Dancy – wouldn't it be better if we had lunch in town?' said Sheena. 'Uncle Malcolm said I had to take you to Wilsons. The lunch there is quite good.'

'I couldn't think of it,' said Mrs Dancy. 'It would cost far too much. But in any case, we couldn't leave poor Annette; she's expecting us.'

SHEENA

'No, of course not,' said Sheena politely, though not very enthusiastically. 'Annette is naturally included in the invitation. It would be my pleasure, Mrs Dancy.'

Mrs Dancy shook her head.

'No,' she said firmly. 'Thank you very much indeed, Sheena, but I think the park would be even nicer. It's such a lovely day, and we can spread my mackintosh on the grass. It will be great fun.'

Sheena looked at her out of those long, slanting, green eyes, as mysterious and unfathomable as the green lochs on her native island, and said no more. One never knew what Sheena MacDonald was thinking . . . At first Mrs Dancy had imagined that the girl was shy and quiet, owing, no doubt, to her solitary childhood; but of late she had begun to wonder if the layer of civilisation the Scots girl had acquired in her Edinburgh school hid a nature as wild, fierce, and – yes, unscrupulous – as that of her kinsmen, the MacDonalds of Sleat, one time Lords of Skye and of the Isles. This particular day something happened that made her sure she was right.

They reached the ballet-school just as the class was ending. Annette, who was talking to the pianist, came forward to meet them, and Miss Brandon smiled affably.

'You've called for Annette? She's ready now. She's been working very hard indeed, haven't you, Annette? Her barre work is improving quite a lot.' She turned away from the newcomers and addressed

145

a group of students who were obviously waiting for instruction. 'Now for your Highland fling. I promised we would run through that, didn't I? You haven't much time to practise it, you know, if the Highland Fair is on Saturday . . .'

'Well, let's go,' said Mrs Dancy. Highland flings weren't much in her line. 'Change quickly, Annette, and bring your case. Come along, Sheena.'

But Sheena stood rooted to the spot. The music playing was a Highland fling, and the students were dancing it rather self-consciously because of the watching visitors. The Scots girl's eyes followed their every movement. When they had finished, she sprang forward.

'That isn't a Highland fling!' she exclaimed. '*That* isn't the way it is danced in Skye! Look – watch me and I will show you how the Highland fling is danced in Armadale Castle in Dunvegan, and everywhere else in the Isle.'

'Sheena, dear –' gasped Mrs Dancy.

'But it's true!' exclaimed the girl passionately. 'It is *not* done like that. May I show you?' She turned to Miss Brandon.

'Certainly, my dear,' said Miss Brandon quietly. She knew enough about girls in general, and dancers in particular, to realise that the one standing before her was something out of the ordinary.

Sheena came alive before their very eyes. This was indeed a new Sheena MacDonald! Her green eyes blazed, her perfect white teeth shone, her kilt swung

round her turned-out knees, her flashing feet beat out
the rhythm in perfect time. No one in Miss Brandon's
studio had seen a Highland fling danced like this! It
wasn't merely a dancer performing a correct Highland fling; it was a Highlander putting into her native
dance all the wild history of her Scottish heritage. All
the mystery of Skye was portrayed in Sheena Mac-
Donald's dancing. Impossible to describe, but
Annette knew that she was watching something quite
perfect. Miss Brandon knew this, too.

'My dear,' she said when it had ended, 'you dance beautifully. Quite beautifully. Where did you learn?'

'I didn't learn,' said Sheena. 'Not in a studio like this –' her eyes swept disdainfully over the room with its mirrors and barres. 'I have always danced my native dances, but I think ballet is silly.'

'Oh!' said Miss Brandon flatly. 'I see.' Then she added, half to herself, 'It seems a shocking waste of talent.'

Mrs Dancy, not being knowledgeable enough to tell one Highland fling from another, said once more, 'We had better be going now, Sheena. I am quite sure Miss Brandon must be tired of watching people dance. Are you ready, Annette?'

Annette ran to collect her things. Going down the stairs to the door she said, as one artiste to another; 'I never saw a Highland fling danced so beautifully, Sheena.'

'Well, you should see Angus, then,' said Sheena. 'He's better than I am.'

'Angus?' repeated Annette. 'I didn't know Angus could dance.'

'Of course he can dance – he's a Highlander,' said Sheena, as if that settled matters.

'How funny. He never told me,' said Annette. 'Fancy me not knowing.'

'I do not think you know a very great deal about Angus,' observed Sheena enigmatically.

5   MAX'S PLAN

Annette wasn't a bit like Sheena when it came to clothes. Apart from her ballet, she didn't care what she wore. Fortunately Aunt Molly usually caught her in time, and Mrs Dancy kept an eye on her daughter's clothes during the holidays. It was: 'Annette! The hem of your skirt has come undone. For goodness' sake, stitch it up, or you'll be tripping up over it.'

Or, Max this time: 'Annette, old girl, your blouse has slipped its moorings. A button or two wouldn't be a bad idea.'

Even Bella got a word in now and again: 'Miss Annette, hinny, what's to dee noo? Your coat has nevor a button on't! Where hast gotten them arl?' Annette would produce four buttons of assorted sizes, shapes, and patterns, and stitch them on the offending garment with any coloured thread that came to hand. Fortunately she didn't bother to look at herself in the glass, so she didn't see how scruffy she looked. . . .

On the other hand, give Annette a few metres of

net and some satin, and she'd turn out a ballet tutu 'of
the most exquisite', as Max put it. Her fingers flew in
and out of the gossamer fabric until she'd produced a
garment fit for a fairy to wear.

Now, if you were going to a party and your mother
suddenly broke the news that you would have to wear
your year-before-last's summer frock, let down, you
might possibly be a little dismayed, and – let's admit
it – disgruntled. Not so Annette.

'Oh, it doesn't matter a bit, Mummy,' she said,
when Mrs Dancy broached the subject. 'After all,
what's a Harvest Home? It's not as if it were a show,
or an exam, or even as if I were dancing –
professionally, I mean. As long as I can have plenty of
net for my new ballet-dress –'

The pucker between Mrs Dancy's brows deepened.

'I'm so sorry, Annette, so dreadfully sorry, but I'm
afraid –' She paused, not knowing how to go on;
how to break the news to her single-minded daughter
that there was to be no new tutu this year at all.

'You're not going to say I can't have one?' burst out
Annette, not very politely, her dream of a tutu snowy
as the breast of a swan in his new plumage vanishing
before her very eyes. 'But Mummy, I must have one!
You don't understand. It isn't like the Children's
Exams, where you go in separately. In the Major
Exams you go in four by four, and the other candi-
dates, in my lot I mean, will *all* have new tutus.
Everyone is having a new tutu.'

'I'm sorry,' repeated Mrs Dancy. 'I just haven't got

a spare penny, Annette. You see, the royalties on Daddy's *Church Through the Middle Ages* have practically stopped altogether, and someone has published a new *Churchgoing in the Seventeenth Century* which makes Daddy's out of date, so they're not going to reprint, and several bills have come in –' She sighed. 'If only I hadn't got that new dress myself, we could have bought the material for your tutu; but I didn't know then that the bills would be so big. I'm afraid we shall have to do without Bella too, and the telephone will have to come out –'

'I can save on food,' said Annette desperately. 'I needn't eat hardly at all.'

'No, you aren't going to starve yourself,' said Mrs Dancy firmly. 'I am not going to allow my family to go short of food, not for a dozen tutus. You can wear your old one, Annette. If your dancing is good enough, it doesn't matter what you wear.'

Annette saw a slow tear rolling down her mother's cheek. She flung herself into Mrs Dancy's arms and broke into wild tears.

'Oh, Mummy, Mummy!' she sobbed. 'Don't worry, I'll manage somehow. I'll manage! We'll all manage – you'll see!' She fled away to the flat roof where she took all her troubles. She found Max there, leaning moodily against the round chimney; he, too, had his problems. He saw immediately that she had been crying.

'What's up, Annette?'

Annette went over to the blackened rampart and

looked out over the wild and desolate moorland. Today the sky was cloudy and full of rain; the weather matched the girl's mood.

'We've no money,' she said simply, and Max, looking at his sister's tear-stained face, knew that, since he had seen her last, Annette had grown up. 'I've just been talking to Mummy, and I can't have a new dress.'

'I didn't know you wanted one,' said Max. 'I didn't know you ever thought about new dresses.'

Annette sighed. 'I mean a ballet-dress.'

'Oh!' There was a long pause. 'Then I suppose it's no use my asking if I can have a new Spanish hat for my next show at the Ballet Workshop.'

'Not the least use,' said Annette. 'After all, your new hat isn't half as important as my tutu.'

'Says you!' commented Max.

There was another long silence.

'Look,' said Max at length, 'there must be some way of making a spot of money. I'm seventeen, and you're nearly fifteen. We're almost grown up.'

But though they thought and thought, they couldn't hit on anything.

'We aren't the sort of people to do the sort of work they want done hereabouts,' observed Max.

Annette giggled.

'I can just see old Adam Robson yelling at us to "Git oot, the pair on ye! Ye're mair bother than ye're worth, both on ye!" But anyway, my exam is at the end of this month.'

'I was forgetting for the moment about your exam. My show –'

'Is next month, and don't I know it!' exploded Annette. 'Haven't you talked of nothing but your old show for weeks on end?'

'Ditto your exam,' retorted Max; 'I'm sick of it!'

'Oh, do stop quarrelling, and let me think,' begged Annette.

'Takes two to quarrel, you know,' said Max, determined to have the last word. Then he gave a shout of triumph. 'I know! I have it!'

'Spit it out,' said Annette inelegantly and without enthusiasm.

'Blackberries!' shouted Max. 'We'll gather them and sell them. Lots in the hedgerows just now.'

There was silence for a short space while the idea sank into Annette's mind. Then she got up.

'Maxie, I believe you're right. It's an idea . . . We gather the blackberries, and sell them in Hexham market place on Tuesday. We'll go shares in the profits – my tutu, your hat. I've got another idea, too.'

'Bet it isn't as good as mine!'

'It's a great deal better,' retorted Annette with dignity.

'Well, what is it?'

'I'll tell you later on, when I've got it worked out,' she promised, and no wheedling on Max's part would make her say another word.

Angus joined in the blackberry picking, too. He happened to be helping his father put some new rose trees in the front garden of the Lodge when Annette and Max went past with their baskets, and of course he wanted to know where they were going.

'Blackberry picking,' said Annette. 'Like to come? The more the merrier! We've got to get as many as possible by tonight. Mummy is coming to help later on – when she's got the housework done. You see, Bella isn't coming any more.'

'Bella not coming any more?' echoed Mr Mac-Crimmon, who had appeared at the french window. 'I thought Bella was a fixture.'

'We've got to economise,' said Annette simply, 'and I need a new tutu.'

Max nudged her sharply and whispered, 'Quiet.' Max didn't think his sister ought to go telling all their family secrets to strangers, even if one of them did happen to be the vicar.

'But surely your mother isn't going to attempt to run that place –' Malcolm MacCrimmon's eyes glanced up at the hoary bulk of Dancing Peel as it towered over the little cottage, and a worried look crept into them '– without any help. It's far too much for one woman to manage.'

'Mummy's pretty tough,' declared Max.

'Yes, I agree she's young and strong,' said the vicar, 'but she's a woman, and that place –'

'You should see Mummy when she's out in the field, creosoting the hen-houses,' put in Annette.

The vicar said no more. He saw that it was well nigh impossible to explain to these two artistic children that their mother hadn't been brought up to scrub stone floors and carry coal. He would see to it that either he or Angus helped her when Max was away. After all, they were neighbours. Aloud he said:

'So you're gathering blackberries to help the family finances? What an excellent idea! I'll come and lend a hand, too, but not just now. I have Matins to say at the church first, you know. I'll join you later.'

'You can come along with Mummy,' said Annette helpfully.

'Yes, I might do that,' agreed the vicar. 'You go with them, Angus, and we'll finish off the rose trees later. By the way,' he added, 'where is Sheena? She might like to go, too. It's a lovely day.'

Sheena was finally tracked down in her bedroom where she was trying on a blouse. When she heard about the blackberrying expedition, she laid down the blouse carefully upon her bed and stared at them.

'Thank you very much,' she said, 'but I do not think I shall come. I might scratch my hands.' She looked down at them – thin, with long, white fingers, slightly cruel.

'Och, and what would it matter if you did?' exploded Angus. 'What is a scratch or two? You are not a film star or a model, are you?'

Sheena didn't answer. In her mind she saw herself treading soft carpets in an exclusive salon – Sheena, the world-famous model! Sheena of the tawny hair and the green eyes – it was an entrancing idea!

'I might be, some day,' she said in her soft, throaty voice.

'I believe that the girl is serious!' said the astounded Angus. Then, as Sheena said no more, he added, 'Oh, well if you won't come, you won't. We're just away – so long!'

'Goodbye,' said Sheena, stroking the glossy, grey-green folds of her blouse. 'It is quite a nice day for blackberrying. What are they for, by the way – jam, or for bottling?'

'Nothing so mundane,' declared Angus. 'They are

for a much more decorative purpose. We are going to sell them to buy some material to make a dress – a ballet-dress for Annette.'

If he had been more observant, he would have seen the narrowing of Sheena's green eyes, the tightening of her small, perfect mouth.

'Really?' she said. 'How romantic! I do hope you get a lot.'

6   ANNETTE'S PLAN

'Two pounds, me; three pounds, you, Angus; Maxie, one-and-a-half pounds,' said Annette, weighing out the gleaming purple berries on the old kitchen scales. 'Your father, one pound – he didn't do as well as I thought he would, and neither did Mummy, but I suppose they had a shorter time. One for Mummy. That's eight-and-a-half pounds altogether. At one pound for a pound it works out to –'

'Eight pounds fifty,' said Angus promptly.

'Thank you,' said Annette. 'But can we charge one pound a pound?'

'It's not enough,' put in Max. 'Eight pounds fifty, I mean. It's only four pounds twenty-five each. Not enough to buy my hat. Besides, there's our bus fare.'

'Never mind,' said Annette. 'It's better than nothing. Perhaps the price of blackberries will have gone up by tomorrow. You never know.'

'Much more likely to have gone down, if you ask me,' said her less optimistic brother.

'Oh, don't be so gloomy, Max!' Annette told him.

'It's always a start, anyway. We can pick some more –'

Max looked down at his hands, criss-crossed with scratches, blotched and sore where the stinging nettles had caught them, stained purple with juice, bitten by midges, and he felt there was something in what Sheena had said – you can pay too high a price for some things! But he had more sense than to say so. Besides, there was Annette's other scheme which she had unfolded to him last night. He felt there might be something in that. They must just wait and see.

Hexham on a market day! A small, grey North-country town with narrow, twisting streets, all leading to a market square, the hub of the town. Round the stalls, jostling each other in high good-humour, milled hundreds of country folk.

Through the short cut, down by the Abbey, poured yet more people, and with them came Annette and her brother, and Angus MacCrimmon, and, last but not least, the eight-and-a-half pounds of blackberries, carefully carried in the washing-up bowl because they couldn't find a basket large enough!

'I do hope we're not too late,' Annette said anxiously.

Alas! The best-laid schemes . . . The price of black-berries had fallen. Moreover, all the market-stall could offer the anxious Dancys was fifty-five pence a pound.

'Ye see,' explained the fresh-faced woman rather apologetically – she liked the look of the two young things – 'we hae oor expenses to meet – the rent and such like. Och, weel, I'll give ye sixty, and that's more than ye'd get at the shops.'

'Thank you,' said Annette sadly. 'It'll just have to do, then. I do see your point about the rent,' she added.

The woman took the blackberries and paid over the money. It came to five pounds twenty-eight pence.

It's no use, thought Annette as they left the stall. Five pounds twenty-eight won't buy even the very cheapest net.

It wouldn't buy the cheapest hat, thought Max.

'It will have to be our other plan,' said Annette aloud. 'What a good thing we thought of it. Come along, Maxie! Let's go back to the bus and collect our things. By the way, where's Angus? He was here a minute ago.'

'He went to do some shopping,' said Max. 'I think we'd better keep it quiet from Angus, Annette, if you don't mind – our plan, I mean. I don't think he'd approve.'

'Neither do I,' said Annette. 'But who cares?' she added wickedly.

The manager of the Regent Cinema was a kind-hearted man. He looked down at the small girl with her little pointed face and sad, dark eyes, and then at the spectacular young man who said he was her brother, and wished that he didn't have to refuse their request. But of course, it was out of the question.

'We don't have "turns",' he explained. 'Ours is a straight cinema show. Our patrons wouldn't like it to be a music hall.'

'They'd like us, though,' pleaded the girl. 'We're good, really we are, and Max learned Spanish dancing under Amaya in Andalusia, and Angelo Andes in London, and Lalagia, and Consuela Carmona, and –'

'It's no use,' said the manager firmly.

'Just watch us,' insisted Annette. 'We're ever so good!'

In a trice a cassette was popped in the player and the manager's office was filled with the haunting rhythm of a flamenco gipsy dance. Curious spectators began to gather at the door to watch the two dancing figures within.

'I agree, you dance very well,' the manager said, and felt he spoke no more than the truth. 'But all the same, it can't be done. I can't employ children, I'm not allowed to.'

'Max is seventeen,' said Annette.

'One of you is no use without the other,' said the manager. 'Anyway,' he added firmly, coming back to his first point, 'we don't have music hall turns in my cinema, as I said before. Sorry, youngsters, but that's final. What are you so keen on doing it for, anyway? Why not wait till you're older?'

'You see, it's now we need the money,' explained Annette. 'Later on it may not be so important. It's for my dress —'

'And for my hat,' put in Max firmly.

Breathlessly the two of them explained, and the manager grew more and more interested. Finally, he dug his hand into his pocket, produced two pounds, and presented one to each of them.

'Here's something to swell the funds,' he said.

'We can't take charity, sir,' said Max.

'This isn't charity,' said the manager. 'It's your due for the excellent performance you have just put up. I can't employ you, for the reasons I gave, but there's nothing to stop me from paying for my seat in the stalls, is there?' He laughed at his own joke. .

'W-ell . . .' Max said doubtfully.

'Thank you most awfully,' said Annette hastily. 'I think perhaps we might take it. It will make all the difference. Come along, Max. You don't mind,' she added to the manager of the cinema, 'if we dance outside?'

'What you do outside isn't any business of mine,' answered the manager with a grin.

'I suppose,' put in Max, 'you haven't a cloakroom or anywhere where we could change into our costumes? We'd be most awfully grateful, sir.'

The manager looked from them to their bags and smiled. He had a small daughter and a son of his own.

'I think I could find somewhere,' he said.

And so it happened that a fascinated crowd in the market square beheld an unexpected display of Spanish dancing. Not many of the spectators were knowledgeable enough to realise that what they were watching was anything more than just 'two kids having a lark', but they knew that they liked it. In a very short time the stalls were deserted, the queue that had formed outside the cinema waiting to go in had turned round and was now facing the opposite way. Quite a few of the queuers had forfeited their places so that they could go on watching the dancing. 'Bravo, kids! Give us another!' they said.

Drivers of cars drew up to see what the crowd was

watching, and stayed to applaud, their passengers leaning out of the windows and clapping. Coins showered into the hat that Max had put on the pavement. It was a triumph!

But, as so often happens with triumphs, it was short-lived. A burly police-constable elbowed his way through the crowd.

'What's going on here?' Imagine his surprise when he finally reached Annette in her frilly skirts, a rose behind one ear! He looked down at her small, sallow face and melting eyes, and then at the boy who stood behind her; the slim, handsome boy in tight black trousers and scarlet bolero. He scratched his head. Never had he come upon anything quite like this!

'A couple o' kids,' he said to himself. Aloud he demanded, 'What's this 'ere? A music 'all? Don't you know you're obstructing the traffic, you two?'

'Oh, are we?' said Annette, her dark eyes as round as saucers. 'Why, so we are – I had no idea we were so popular!'

The constable looked at her suspiciously. No, she was not being cheeky.

Just at this moment, a tall figure forged his way from the outskirts of the crowd and stood beside them.

'Angus!' cried Annette, with a sigh of relief. 'Do tell him we're not criminals.'

Angus took in the situation at a glance. He felt like laughing, but he managed to keep a straight face.

'Annette, you naughty girl!' he exclaimed. After all,

it might be a good thing if the policeman thought Annette was twelve years old, instead of nearly fifteen! 'Come away this minute! I'm so sorry, Inspector. I ought to have been looking after them.'

'So you're her brother, eh?' said the constable, relenting a little. 'Well, you're not much alike, but I'll take your word for it. Now I'll give you a word of advice, sonny. Get her out of here, and the other kid, too –' this being Max who was a year older than Angus '– and keep your eye on them in future, and there'll be no more said. I don't want to be hard on kids.'

He strode away through the crowd which was rapidly thinning now that there seemed to be no prospect of further entertainment.

'Oh, Angus, he hasn't taken our collection!' cried Annette with a sigh of relief. 'I was so afraid he would. I don't believe he realised it was there. It looks like quite a lot of money.'

Angus looked down at the hat with its pile of coins. 'You ought to give it back, you know,' he said severely. 'You have no right to go begging, Annette. It was very naughty of you both – really, I'm surprised at Max.'

'It wasn't begging,' argued Annette. 'We were entertaining the crowd, just as they used to do in the days of Queen Elizabeth and Shakespeare.'

Angus had no answer to this.

'Anyway,' said Annette triumphantly, 'we can't give it back now. They're all gone!'

And, sure enough, as she spoke, the last member of the cinema queue disappeared into the Regent, and the last interested shopper melted away.

'It's funny,' said Annette, as she folded up her Spanish petticoats carefully – they belonged to Miss Brandon and, since they were stage property, they must be treated with respect. Her own clothes had been bundled into her case all anyhow, and now, when she put them on, she looked 'a proper sketch', as Bella would have put it. 'It's funny how things always work out if you make up your mind hard enough.'

'It certainly seems to work that way with you,' said Max, looking at his sister with admiration. 'Well, what do we do now?'

'Ballet net,' answered Annette. 'Let's see if they have any at Cartrights.' She fastened her case and crammed her hat over her hair. 'We'll just manage to get in before they close, if we're quick.'

'You're not forgetting my hat, I hope?' put in Max anxiously. He knew Annette and her one-track mind.

'N-no, of course not.'

'Fair shares,' added Max.

'Fair shares,' agreed Annette reluctantly.

'Thanks a lot,' said Max. 'I shall have to send away to London for my hat, of course. Here you are, then.' He handed a handful of money over to his sister. 'Your share of the loot!'

Any other boy would have stayed outside the shop while Annette made her purchases. Angus did, anyway. But not so Max. He not only went in with her, but stood beside her, feeling the net between his fingers, and offering suggestions. The shop assistants were fascinated, and soon quite a crowd of them had gathered round the two young dancers. It was a good thing it was just on closing time so there weren't many customers.

'I'm so happy! I'm so happy!' exclaimed Annette, doing an entrechat as they left the shop, to the delight of the passers-by. 'Think of the gorgeous tutu I shall be able to make with all that net. Now for the satin. What a pity they hadn't the right sort there. It would have saved a lot of trouble.'

They got the satin at Armstrongs. You might think that satin is satin all the world over and that so long as it was white, it didn't matter which one they bought. You have much to learn! Annette discarded roll after roll. 'Too shiny . . . Too metallic . . . Too thin . . . Oh, that one's lovely! How much is it? . . . Oh, I see, slipper satin . . . I'm afraid we can't possibly afford . . . you see we've only got . . .'

At last they managed to get half a metre of satin that looked good but was actually quite cheap, and Max put the small parcel in his pocket. Annette insisted upon carrying the net herself.

'You might squash it,' she said, when he offered to take it. 'You'd be thinking of your zapateado!'

So back they went in the bus in triumph, having rejoined Angus outside the shop. Although they had to stand most of the way and they were both tired after their strenuous afternoon, they were blissfully happy. As they joggled along the winding country roads, Annette dreamed about the beautiful white tutu she would make which could charm the stony hearts of the examiners. Why, she might even get honours! Max thought of the dashing hat he would have for his next Spanish show.

7   HARVEST HOME

Everyone from far and near came to the Mintlaw Harvest Home. It was held towards the end of September, after the harvest was safely in.

Of course there was an enormous supper, spread out on trestle tables in the adjoining school room. It consisted entirely of home-made cakes, scones, 'singing hinnies', sausage rolls, and all those good things that make north-country cooking famous, and was contributed by the whole parish.

Before the festivities began, everyone congregated at the little stone church for the Harvest Festival service. The church had been decorated that morning by a band of enthusiasts, led by Mrs Dancy and Lady Fenwick from Colburn Hall.

The service was at half past six and, as the Harvest Home began at eight o'clock, most of the people came to church dressed ready for the evening. Sheena wore her new green coat with a green velvet dress underneath. Annette's school coat hid the faded cotton dress that was the only garment she had suitable for an evening of dancing. Mrs Dancy wore the new dress she had made herself.

The old church was lit by hanging lanterns and candles had been lit in brass sconces on the walls. In the middle of the sanctuary hung a beautiful old brass candelabrum polished to satiny brightness, and holding thirty candles which winked every time the church door opened to admit yet another family, or whenever the vicar passed underneath and caused a draught.

As the new vicar looked round his church and saw it decorated for his first Harvest Thanksgiving, he gave a sigh of happiness. It was amazing that so many flowers could have been grown in the little cottage gardens!

Mrs Dancy was thinking how artistic the long trails and tendrils of scarlet Virginia creeper looked, hanging from the lectern, which had been her work that morning, and also how nice the new vicar looked in the snowy surplice that she had washed and ironed for him only yesterday. Annette was counting the number of days before her exam, and wondering how many classes she could manage to get in before then. Sheena MacDonald – who knew what Sheena MacDonald was thinking?

Max was remembering with a thrill of joy the sleek black lines of his Spanish hat which had arrived in a large box from the theatrical dealers only that morning. Angus was wondering if he should take his pony to be shod the next day, or leave it until the day after.

He was also thinking about the coming dance, and how he would dance with Annette for the first time. An eightsome reel, it would be, he decided. Perhaps a foursome, too.

The service went off beautifully, and everyone enjoyed the Harvest hymns, the words of which they all knew by heart.

The night wore on. The windows of the village hall grew wet and steamy as the crowd inside grew larger. The band warmed up and, in local language, 'fair took the roof off' with their reels and Border dances, and the hall echoed with the whoops and yells of the dancers. It was all very free and easy, and also very friendly. Everybody danced with everybody, no matter who they were. Even the aloof Sheena enjoyed herself – it was quite like her native ceilidh. In her green dress she knew she was looking beautiful and she got all the dances. Annette, on the other hand, got very few. Possibly it was because no one really knew whether she was a child or a grown-up – fifteen was considered grown up in the village – or possibly it was because of her slightly haughty manner. Or again, Sheena may have had something to do with it, if her conversation with Angus was a fair sample of her conversation with her other partners.

'Yes, isn't it a pity,' said Sheena, as they danced together, 'that Annette is so frightfully bad at ballroom dancing?'

Angus stared at her.

'What is it that you are meaning?'

'I should not think it needed me to explain,' went on Sheena. 'She may be very good at her ballet but she cannot dance an ordinary quickstep.'

'Who wants her to?' exploded Angus hotly. He thought Annette's every movement was grace and perfection and would not allow any one else to say a word against her. 'I think she dances beautifully,' he declared. 'You must be mad to think otherwise.'

Sheena said no more. She saw it was no use talking to Angus about Annette's dancing. He was certainly bewitched, just as his ancestor, Black Lad, had been bewitched by a fairy who had given him, as a love-token, the gift of music . . . She tried another tack. 'Then there's her dress,' she said. 'Awful isn't the word!'

'They are hard up,' said Angus. 'The Dancys, I mean. It isn't Annette's fault.'

'Of course not,' said Sheena smoothly. 'It is a great pity, though, for anyone to look so untidy. I think she might sew on one or two buttons.'

Annette felt that there was something wrong, too. Until this night, until the moment when she had caught sight of herself in a long mirror that stood by the stage, she had never cared what she looked like, or even thought about it, except in a theatrical performance, of course. But now, when she saw herself standing with Angus, side by side with Sheena and her brother, waiting to begin the eightsome reel, she felt a throb of envy. There was Sheena, in her green velvet dress, her red-gold hair brushed until it shone and glowed like burnished copper, her beautiful white skin, her long, mysterious eyes . . . Next to her stood a rather forlorn little figure – Annette Dancy, in her dress of no particular colour and of no particular shape. It was too short; it was skimpy. In fact, thought Annette, it was only fit for a jumble sale! Her hair was all wrong, too. It was too heavy for her face, it was rough, it looked as if it had never seen a hairbrush, unkempt was the only word for it!

Still, on the whole, Annette enjoyed herself. She was quite content to sit and watch other people dancing waltzes and quicksteps as long as she was able to dance the other sort, and both Max and Angus saw to it that she did that. Angus was indeed a wonderful Scottish dancer, and he and Annette attracted a great deal of attention as they led the eightsome reel, putting in all the intricate little steps that make such a difference to the dance. Even Annette's faded print dress couldn't hide her grace.

Everyone was there, and if you had gone round Mintlaw village on that September night you would have found it deserted. Even old Sally's Timmy was away from home. She had found a way into the schoolroom through a small window at the back, and was busily licking the cream off the top of the trifles. Yes, Timmy was quite up to a Border raid now and again, even if she had only three legs!

A slight sound from the window disturbed her. She looked up, amber eyes gleaming, whiskers twitching. The sound came again. Then a small furry

head appeared round the edge of the window frame; two innocent kitten eyes looked into Timmy's own.

Timmy got back to business again and when a chattering, laughing group of supper-seekers appeared in the doorway, cat and kitten slid noiselessly to the floor and disappeared. In the heat of the moment, no one noticed that the cream on the trifles was a little disarranged . . .

8   DISASTER!

Yes, Mintlaw was indeed a deserted village that night. Only one intruder was abroad, and no one saw him stealing round Dancing Peel as he carried out his business. He did what he had come to do, and no one was any the wiser until next morning when Mrs Dancy went to let out and feed her hens. She came back white-faced.

'We've had a visit from the fox,' she said to Annette, who was busy cooking the breakfast. Her words might not have conveyed much to a town-dweller, but Annette knew only too well what they meant.

'The pullets – the cock-chickens –'

'He's killed the lot,' said poor Mrs Dancy, sitting down on the nearest chair. 'There must have been two foxes, I think. Of course, it's all my own fault; I forgot to shut them in last night. It was the Harvest Home . . .'

When Annette went out to inspect the damage, she found all her mother's fat pullets, just on the point of laying, and all her cock-chickens, meant for the Christmas market, lying dead in neat rows. The thief, or thieves, as the case might be, had only actually taken away two pullets, but had made sure that no one else should have the rest. He had neatly bitten off all their heads; the ground was covered with feathers, a sad reminder of the mass slaughter . . .

You might have thought that Annette would have revised her views on hunting, but not so! 'He didn't know any better,' she declared through her tears. As I said before, Annette stuck to her principles, whether it suited her or not.

The affair was little short of a tragedy. To Mrs Dancy, her poultry was her living. Mr Dancy's books, now bringing in only a small amount each year and not likely to do that much longer, and Mrs Dancy's clergy widow's pension were now all that stood between the Dancy family and poverty. Clearly something must be done. All day long Mrs Dancy turned over in her mind the pros and cons of the matter. The loss of her precious hens just ended everything. In short, the Dancys were living beyond their means. Something must surely be done about it.

All night long, Mrs Dancy tossed and turned in bed and tried to see a way out of her troubles; all the next day she debated with herself until, eventually, she had quite made up her mind.

'We must leave here,' she said. 'I've been thinking about it for a while, and now I have quite decided.

We can't afford to stay here any longer. I must get some work to do.'

The two Dancy children were so horrified at their mother's words that for several minutes they sat, as if turned to stone, saying nothing.

'You don't mean leave Dancing Peel, Mummy?' burst out Annette at length.

'I'm sorry,' said Mrs Dancy, as though it was her fault. 'I know how you both feel about it. I know how you hate the idea, especially since we'd just got things nicely settled – about the new vicarage, and every-thing. I hate it, myself. But you see how it is, darlings. I shall simply have to get a job as a housekeeper or a matron in a school. There must be something I can do. I don't mind how hard I work. Perhaps I could look after a clergy rest-house, then I should be able to have the two of you to live with me in the holidays.'

Max stood up. He seemed to have grown older in the last few moments. 'Don't make any plans for me, Mama,' he said quietly. 'I know I'm supposed to be going on to university after I leave school but, as a matter of fact, I'm not. I'm joining a company of Spanish dancers right away.'

'Max!' exclaimed Mrs Dancy.

'Yes, really, Mama,' repeated Max firmly. 'I've been wondering how to break it to you. You see, even if I go to university it would still be years and years before I got my degree, and what should we live on during that time? There would be my fees –'

'You could get a grant,' said Mrs Dancy faintly.

'Not a hope!' said Max. 'Not enough, anyway. And it would be an awful waste because I should just go off dancing in the end. I'm a dancer, Mama! I know it, and you do too, only you won't admit it. Well, now it's decided. I shall join Teresa and Luisillo straight away. I can get in – they said so. I had an audition when they were up here. So you see how it is, Mama. Anyway,' he added, 'I shall be able to help financially.' At seventeen, Max was to get exactly twice what poor Mr Dancy received as his clerical income, after a lifetime of devoted work!

'And I shall get an RAD scholarship!' put in Annette. 'I simply must get one! I'll get honours in my exam, and then I'll get –' She went on building castles in the air, and her mother and brother listened to her in amazement.

'You mustn't expect too much, darling,' said Mrs Dancy cautiously.

'But I must do it – I *must*!' repeated Annette. 'We'll manage somehow.' This had always been her cry whenever things grew too bad. She refused to be beaten. And very often they had 'managed somehow', but this time Mrs Dancy felt that the odds were too heavily against her. Annette probably wouldn't win her scholarship – one usually didn't if one wanted it so badly. That was Mrs Dancy's experience of life, anyhow . . . And as for the other dreams, well, only time would show if they were ever to become reality.

'I know you'll do your best,' she said gently, 'but don't build up too many hopes, darling. You see, even if Max can contribute a little, and you do well in your exam, we may still not be able to go on living here. I've been thinking for a long time –'

'We can't leave Dancing Peel, Mummy – we *can't*!' cried Annette wildly. 'I should die!' She rushed out of the room, banging the door behind her and nearly colliding with Sheena, who was standing outside. She was all dressed up in riding-clothes, but Annette was too het-up to be surprised.

'I'm so sorry – I'm afraid I heard what you said. You were talking rather loudly,' said Sheena. 'Surely you aren't thinking of leaving the peel?'

'No, of course not!' flashed Annette. 'It was just something Mummy said, and it was the most stupid idea I ever heard of. As if we could possibly leave Dancing Peel! Why, it's our peel; it's our home.'

'It's really the vicarage, you know,' observed Sheena. 'If it belongs to anybody, it belongs to us.'

'We've been paying rent for it,' said Annette.

'I know you have,' agreed Sheena. 'Uncle Malcolm said at the very beginning he supposed he would have to accept a nominal rent so that your mother wouldn't feel under too much of an obligation, but of course it wasn't worth it, really. I mean, it's been very awkward for Uncle having to live in that small cottage – you must see that, Annette. All his friends thought it was very strange indeed, when there was a perfectly good vicarage there all the time. Angus was saying only last night –' She stopped abruptly. No one knew better than Sheena the value of a sentence left unfinished.

'*What* was Angus saying?' demanded Annette dangerously.

Sheena shrugged her shoulders.

'Oh, it was nothing. I think I had better not tell you; it might make you angry. You are such a firework, you know, Annette. Of course, as I told Angus, we couldn't possibly turn your poor mother out, but if you really are going to leave of your own accord, it would settle everything.'

'But we're *not*!' flashed Annette. 'I've just told you!'

'Oh! Then it was my mistake,' Sheena said smoothly. 'And poor Angus will just have to go on taking Black Bess all that way up to the Coldburn stables, because there is only room for my uncle's horse at the Lodge, and you –'

'I didn't ask him to take his beastly pony to Coldburn Hall,' burst out Annette. 'It was his own idea. I told him he could have his old stable, and I would dance somewhere else.'

'You were not very gracious about it, were you?' said Sheena. 'After the way you said it, you couldn't really blame Angus.'

'I'm not blaming him!' shouted the goaded Annette. 'Why should I bother to blame him? I hate him, anyway!' It wasn't the truth. She didn't hate Angus. She liked him very much indeed, in spite of everything. That was what hurt – the thought that Angus had talked over her faults and failings with Sheena. 'Oh, go away!' she said.

'But I want to see your mother.'

Just as this moment the door opened, and Mrs Dancy appeared. She looked from one to the other.

'I thought I heard someone shouting. Oh, it's you, Sheena. Is anything the matter, dear?'

'Nothing,' said Sheena calmly. 'I just came over to say goodbye – for the present, I mean. I am going

home to Glendounie for a few days before I go back
to school, and Uncle is going with me. He has some
business to see to in Portree, some houses he wishes
to sell. We are going to Fort William by the midnight
train, and Sir William is sending us in to Newcastle in
his car – it's more reliable than ours! I am taking my
pony over to Coldburn now; Sir William lent him to
me, you know. That's why I'm dressed like this.' She
glanced down at her riding-clothes.

'You mean you're going all the way back to Skye?'
said Mrs Dancy. 'It seems a very long way, Sheena!'

'Oh, no, Mrs Dancy,' answered Sheena. 'It is not so
very far. We shall be there by tomorrow night. Uncle
said I was to tell you he'd be back at the end of the
week, and if anyone wanted the vestry key, he's left it
with old Mr Hindhaugh, the churchwarden, and he's
arranged with Mr Livingstone, of Tarset, to look
after the parish while he's away. Uncle was very sorry
he couldn't come himself, but he had to go over to
Whinshiel to see old Mrs Mouncy. She's going into
hospital tomorrow and he wanted to see her before
she went. He's joining me at Coldburn later on
tonight.'

'It's all very sudden,' declared Mrs Dancy. 'Do
come in, Sheena. It's very cold, standing out
there.'

'No, thank you very much,' said the girl. 'I mustn't
stay. Yes, it is a bit sudden. You see, they rang up
about the houses only this evening, and it seemed too
good an opportunity for us not to go together.'

'You love Skye?' said Mrs Dancy, struck by the expression on the girl's face.

'It is my home,' Sheena told her simply. Even Annette, prejudiced as she was, felt that whatever Sheena's faults and failings, she was passionately fond of the island of her birth.

'Well, if both you and your uncle are going off tonight,' said Mrs Dancy, 'what about Angus? Is he going, too?'

'Oh, no! Angus is staying here,' said Sheena. 'You see, he goes back to school on Saturday – not a week later, like me. Besides, there is the meet of the hounds at Coldburn tomorrow. He would not like to miss that.'

'Then he must certainly stay here with us,' said Mrs Dancy. 'We couldn't think of the poor boy living all by himself down at the Lodge. Would you tell him, Sheena, please – oh, but of course you can't, if you're on your way to Coldburn now. Never mind, Annette will go, won't you, Annette?'

'All right, Mummy,' said Annette. Although outwardly polite, she was seething inwardly with indignation. All Angus cared about was chasing things, and discussing her faults and failings with the perfect Sheena.

'Well, goodbye, Mrs Dancy,' said Sheena, holding out her hand. 'I expect I shall be seeing you next holidays. I usually spend part of them with Uncle Malcolm and Angus. Please say goodbye to Max for me.'

185

Warm-hearted Mrs Dancy kissed her.

'Goodbye, darling. Have a good journey,' she said. Then a thought struck her. 'Did you say you were riding over to Coldburn tonight, Sheena? It's as dark as the inside of your hat.'

'Oh, that's all right,' Sheena declared. 'I'm quite used to riding round in the dark. I often do at home. I have a flashlight. Anyway, it's such a stormy night, I don't expect there will be much on the road.'

It occurred to Mrs Dancy, not for the first time, that in spite of her decorative appearance, Sheena was quite a tough young woman.

9   STORM

Meanwhile, Annette had slipped on wellingtons and a mackintosh, and splashed down the overgrown drive to the Lodge. It was raining harder than ever. There was a light in the window, and sounds of an orchestra. She tried the front door but it was locked, so she ran round to the back and, finding the kitchen door open, she walked in. Annette crossed the kitchen and knocked on the sitting-room door.

'Come in!' said a voice with a note of surprise in it. Then the surprise turned to pleasure, 'Oh, it is you, Annette. Come in. You are just in time to hear Beethoven's Ninth . . .' He got up and crossed the room in a couple of strides.

'I've only come to tell you that Mother says you can come and stay with us while your father is away, if you like,' said Annette stiffly. She was aware that her words didn't sound very gracious, but then she wasn't feeling gracious. She was still remembering Sheena's words . . .

Meanwhile Angus had turned down the music

until the orchestra sounded faint and far away, as if heard in a dream.

'That is nice of her. And you, Annette? Do you want me to stay with you?'

How like Angus, thought Annette, to put her in an awkward position. Any other boy would have accepted and had done with it. Not so Angus! He was waiting for her to say she wanted him too. Well, she didn't – not now!

'You can if you wish,' she said coldly.

Angus stared at her for a long moment.

'I am thinking that I shall not be accepting your mother's kind invitation,' he said in his soft Highland voice. 'I shall be quite all right here. Will you please thank her for me, all the same.'

'All right,' said Annette. Now that he had declined the invitation, she wished he had accepted. 'Are you quite sure?'

'I am quite sure,' Angus said quietly.

'Oh! Then I'll go. Goodnight, Angus.'

He murmured something she didn't understand. 'What did you say?'

'I am only bidding you goodnight in the Gaelic, Annette.'

'Why in the Gaelic?'

'It suits my mood.' He turned up the music again and Annette felt she was dismissed. He came out with her and opened the door, the front door, this time. He treated her as if she were a stranger.

'Goodnight, Annette.'

'Goodnight, Angus.'

As she ran back up the drive, she thought: He hasn't wished me luck for my exam. He knows it's tomorrow. All he's thinking about is his horrid hunt – and getting rid of us!

A fitful moon came out from behind a ragged belt of cloud and shone for a moment on the stable door. A wicked thought came into Annette's head. She'd spoil his hunt for him. She'd maybe spoil his hunting altogether, and serve him right! She'd show him!

She ran to the stable door and looked inside. Yes, there was Black Bess. She was clipped trace-high, and the top half of her was like soft black velvet, while underneath she gleamed liked satin. It was evident

that Angus had done his best to have her looking her best for tomorrow's meet.

'I'll show him!' repeated Annette to herself. She opened the door and stood back. Black Bess whinnied softly and came towards her, keen to leave the boredom of her stable. Annette wanted to take to her heels in headlong flight, but she took stern hold of herself. She opened the little door in the wall of the stable-yard that gave directly on to the moor, and shooed the pony through it.

When Black Bess felt the springy turf under her hoofs she kicked up her heels and was away. Annette watched her vanish into the darkness like a shadowy phantom. The moon had retreated behind its cloud once more. Silence reigned. The deed was done . . .

Annette walked soberly back to the house. As usual, the moment she had done anything wicked, she wished she hadn't done it; how she wished she could bring the pony back into the stable.

Mrs Dancy noticed that her daughter was rather thoughtful and absent-minded during supper, but put it down to the effects of their conversation earlier in the day. Max, who knew his sister rather better, stared at her thoughtfully for quite a long time, and then remarked, 'Annette, do you know you've eaten a whole slice of bread without any butter on it. Are you economising, or what? Or are you scared of getting fat? Shouldn't think it very likely, myself.'

Annette looked up, and he could see by her startled expression that her thoughts had been miles and miles away. 'Butter?' she repeated vaguely.

'Yes, butter,' said Max. 'Stuff produced by the cow. Usually put on bread.'

'I-I must have been thinking of something else,' said Annette, blushing furiously.

'That had occurred to me, too,' observed Max. 'Thought to myself: "Kid sister ruminating on evil doings." Come on, Annette – what have you been up to?'

'Nothing, nothing at all,' declared Annette. She wasn't going to tell Max, or her mother, or anyone, about her escapade that evening. She went upstairs to bed, telling herself firmly, over and over again, that Angus deserved it. He deserved it!

The moment she reached her bedroom and switched on the light on her bedside table, she saw that there was something on her pillow. It was a note which said: *I am wishing you the very best of luck for tomorrow – Angus.* And beside it lay a piece of white heather.

'Oh, Angus!' sobbed Annette, flinging herself face downwards on the bed. 'Oh, Black Bess! What have I done? I'm a wicked, wicked girl!' The soft patter of the raindrops on the windowpane sounded to her like tears falling.

All night long it rained. How it rained! And all night long Annette tossed and turned and couldn't go to sleep. Or if she did sleep, she dreamt of dreadful things, like floods and runaway horses. Once, half asleep, she ran over to the window and looked out. As she stood there, the sky was cleft by forked lightning and thunder rolled dully, whilst all the time the rain came down in sheets and torrents. In the greenish glare of the lightning flash she saw below her the Mintlaw burn, brown, turbulent, menacing.

It's almost burst its banks, thought Annette. She had never seen it so high. Out there in the rain and the darkness, thought Annette, was poor Black Bess. In her imagination she heard a frightened neigh but, though she strained her eyes, she couldn't see anything moving in the blackness outside. Once she thought of dressing and going down to the Lodge, and telling Angus what she had done. She even got up and began putting on her shoes and socks, then took them off again; for what could she, or Angus, or anyone do, while it was still dark? She must just wait until morning. She looked at her watch. Only three o'clock!

A few minutes later, or so it seemed, there was a knock on her door, and Max's voice, sharp with anxiety, shouted, 'Annette! Get up! It's seven o'clock, and the most awful thing's happened!'

She bundled on her clothes in the half-dark, shivering with cold. Outside, the dawn was coming, and she could see that the rain had stopped at last and the sun was rising. In the east the sky was a pale primrose colour and a wan, washed-out star or two still twinkled. She went to the window and gave a gasp. Outside in the dim light was nothing but water. A sheet of water. The peel-tower stood, as it were, in the middle of the sea. Glimmering eerily in the sunrise, water splashed gently against the very walls of the old building.

Annette dashed down the stairs, nearly falling headlong in her haste.

'Mummy! Mummy!'

Her mother, Max and Bella stood with pale faces on the threshold of the kitchen. Inside, rippling up to their feet, was a waste of water. Chairs, table, and even the oak settle, floated on it, gently rocking to and fro, as if they were boats.

'There's bin a flood,' said Bella in her broadest Northumbrian. 'Aye, there's a deal o' watter in this 'ere kitchen, but it's naught to what there is ootside! Near drooned some on us ha' been, and aal the briggs swept awa'.'

It was a few moments before the significance of these words dawned upon Annette. Then she grabbed Bella by the arm.

'Bridges washed away? You don't mean – you don't mean, Bella, that there won't be any buses?'

'Buses?' echoed Bella, looking down at the anxious face on a level with her own broad shoulder. 'Buses, Miss Annette? Not wi'oot they're on floats, like them flying boats, or like the Ark i' the Bible!'

'But how am I to get to Newcastle?' wailed Annette.

'Ye canna get into Newcastle,' declared Bella. 'Not unless ye swim.' She nodded over her shoulder towards the window. 'And then ye'd be drooned in yon ragin' roarin' watter. Ye'd best bide at hame, Miss Annette.'

'But it's my exam!'

'Oh, Annette, do shut up about your stupid exam!' exclaimed Max, who was standing there in his dressing-gown, his black hair on end. 'There are worse things than your exam, I can tell you! Angus has lost Black Bess. She's been washed away.'

'Oh, no!' said Annette faintly. 'She can't have been! It can't be true!'

'Well, it is,' repeated Max. 'Angus was here a few

minutes ago and he was in a frightful state. He shut
Bess in the stable up here as usual last night and went
to bed, never thinking that during the night the stable
would be washed away.'

'Oh!' said Annette, with a white face. 'It can't be
true!'

'When he woke,' went on Max, 'he looked out of
the window and saw at once what had happened, so
he rushed up here. Goodness knows how he got here
– the drive is under half a metre of water. He found a
huge gap in the stable wall, and a raging torrent
tearing through, and no pony there at all. The door
was open, so the poor beast had evidently been
washed right through it, and goodness only knows
where she is by now. He thinks she'll be drowned, for
sure.'

'Poor Angus,' said Mrs Dancy. 'He was nearly out
of his mind. He loves his pony so dearly. I tried to
persuade him to have some breakfast before he went
out to look for her, but he wouldn't even have a cup
of tea.'

'Oh, why didn't he come and tell me,' said Annette.
'Why didn't he?'

They all stared at her.

'Tell you?' said Mrs Dancy. 'But what good would
that have done? You couldn't have done anything.'

'I might have been able to – you never know,'
moaned Annette. 'Oh, poor, poor Angus!'

It was at this moment that Angus himself appeared. His face was wreathed in smiles.

'She's all right!' he shouted. 'They've found her! And where do you think she was! On that bit of high ground behind the peel! She must have swum there. She always was a wise old girl. The odd thing is that there's no mud on her and you'd think, after swimming through all that – but never mind, she's safe, and that's all that matters. I'll have some breakfast now, please, Mrs Dancy, if there's any left.'

They all sat down in the Round Lounge and ate the meal Bella had cooked. Annette was very silent.

Poor child! thought her mother. The news about Angus's pony has upset her. It must have been a terrible shock. It certainly had been, though not quite in the way Mrs Dancy meant!

If I hadn't done what I did, thought Annette, Black Bess would have been drowned. And I spent nearly all night wishing I hadn't done it!

'Bella says the bridges have been swept away,' she said at length. 'It isn't true, is it?'

'It's true enough,' said Angus. 'But I've been thinking, now that Bess is safe, we may be able to do something about it. About your exam, I mean. The RSPCA man – I phoned him about Bess – well, he says there isn't a hope of getting through by car or bus, and the AA confirmed that. Neither of them can get through until the floods subside.'

'Then how . . .' said Annette faintly. She was seized by a horrible, sick feeling, the sort of feeling you get when you know something awful is going to happen, and you can't do anything to stop it.

'There's a chance we might get through, I'm not promising, mind you, but we might manage it on horseback,' said Angus. 'If you're game, that is.'

'You mean – *ride* through the water? On *Bess*?'

'That's the general idea. You can ride in front of me, and when we come to where the bridges aren't, I'll wade and lead her across. It's just possible, provided we can find places to cross where the water isn't too deep. All your things are in Newcastle, aren't they? Your frilly what's-its-name, and so on?'

'Annette took her tutu in on Saturday,' said Mrs Dancy. 'But Angus, won't it be very dangerous?'

'I won't let her risk her life, Mrs Dancy,' said Angus with a smile, 'if that's what you mean. If it's a case of that, we'll give it up, you can depend upon me. But I think I know how to get through.'

'Come on – let's go quickly!' exclaimed Annette. 'My exam is at two.'

'Sorry to have to leave you with all this to clear up,' apologised Angus. 'I'll come back and lend a hand when I've got Annette to the nearest bus.' And off they went.

10 THE EXAM

It was a nightmare ride. Poor Black Bess, having spent all those hours out in the wind and the rain, not to mention a freak thunderstorm, wanted to go back to her warm stable – for how was she to know that her stable was now more like the bed of a stream? – and Angus had to dismount and lead her by the bridle most of the way. Sometimes he even had to use his crop as well as his voice to urge her onwards. In places the ground was so boggy that Angus sank in nearly to the top of his wellingtons, and it took him all his time to stagger along. Even when he was able to ride, the cold wind chilled him through and through, and Annette's cheeks were blue with the cold. The only bright spot in the whole dismal business was the fact that with every muddy field they crossed, and every swollen burn, they drew nearer to civilisation and the all-important bus.

'Now we come to the stiffest part,' declared Angus. 'Here's where we have to cross the Tarret burn.'

When Annette saw the raging torrent in front of them and thought of all that Angus had done for her, just so that she shouldn't miss a dancing exam that, after all, didn't mean a thing to him, her conscience smote her.

'Angus,' she said. 'I want to tell you something. I did a dreadful thing last night. *I* let Black Bess out of the stable. I did it on purpose – I wanted to hurt you.'

Angus was busy urging his reluctant pony into the flooded stream, where he judged the water wasn't too

deep. How like Annette, he thought, to start confessing at a moment such as this.

'I shall hear all about that some other time,' he said. 'Come on, Bess, old girl. Gently does it. Come on, now.'

'Angus! You aren't listening – you don't understand. It was I who . . .'

Angus grinned up at her. Now that his beloved pony was safe and sound, no mere wickedness on Annette's part could worry him. 'If you would just be quiet until we have crossed this stream, and until you have caught your bus –'

'But I want to tell you –'

'You shall do so later on,' Angus assured her gently. They had got safely over to the other side by this time. 'Then I shall listen to you.'

Annette looked down at him. It occurred to her that perhaps Sheena was right, and that she didn't know a very great deal about Angus MacCrimmon.

They reached Bellingham, weary and mudstained, at a quarter to eleven. People stared at them curiously, rather as if they were two strange beings from another planet. The storm was on everyone's lips. AA and RAC men patrolled the streets, putting signs up in the flooded areas: LOOP-ROAD, DANGER, DIVERSION, BRIDGE DOWN, ROAD BLOCKED ONE MILE, TAKE SIDE ROAD HALF-MILE ON LEFT, and other instructions. If Angus and Annette hadn't been so weary, they would have been thrilled.

'I hope you won't be too tired for your exam,' Angus said anxiously, looking at his companion's small white face. 'You will get some lunch in town?'

'Oh, yes,' Annette assured him. 'I expect I shall forget about being tired when I'm in my exam.' As a matter of fact, the ride over the flooded fields and moorland wasn't really the cause of the drawn look on her face. It was the mental strain she had been through, and the sleepless night she had spent.

'Well, goodbye, Annette,' said the boy, as they reached the bus station and he helped her down from the pony's back. 'The best of luck! I hope you get your honours all right.'

Annette climbed into the waiting bus and said, 'Goodbye, Angus! What will you do now? Will you ride back over all those fields again?'

He shook his head. 'No, I think Bess has had enough for one day,' he answered. 'I shall stable her here and come back for her later on. As for me, I shall stay here for a short time and talk to the AA men. They may be able to get through, and I shall beg a lift.'

The bus-driver revved his engine as a warning to late-comers that his bus was about to depart. Annette leaned perilously out of the door.

'Angus!'

He swung himself into the saddle and rode alongside as the bus pulled out on to the road.

'What is it?'

'I forgot to say thank you, Angus!'

He laughed and dropped behind. The bus got up

speed, turned a corner, and he was gone. Annette's lips set in a firm line. Another hurdle lay in front of her, a hurdle she must clear herself with no help from anybody, her exam, on whose result so many things depended.

As Annette had said, she forgot all her weariness when she was dressed for her exam. Moreover, the gasps of admiration that greeted her when she came out of the dressing-room and walked into the small practice-room, where the candidates waited their turn to go into the big studio for their ordeal, would have refreshed an even more weary person than Annette Dancy:

'Oh, Annette, what a perfectly gorgeous tutu!'

'Did you have it made at Scotts, Annette?'

'What, you made it yourself? I just don't believe it!'

'You'll make the rest of us look like ugly ducklings, all right, Annette!'

The exam was like a dream to Annette. She remembered doing the well-known barre-work in the well-known studio to the well-known RAD music. She remembered a long table with a keen-eyed woman sitting at it making notes and, beside her, a little man with tousled hair and glittering black eyes staring at her. She remembered working out difficult *enchaîne-ments*, and getting them right – she thought – trying her hardest to 'turn out from the hips' when she executed an arabesque, a développé, her mind sending frantic signals to her aching legs.

There was a pause, while those who wished could

change from unblocked shoes to blocked, but most of the students, including Annette, wore blocked shoes all the time.

Annette's point-work was good. She had strong, elegant feet, with highly arched insteps; but again she was straining to achieve the necessary turned-out line. The examiners scribbled away on their forms as the exam drew to an end. They asked a few questions on technique, and it was over. The four of them were once more back in the little practice-room, and it was the turn of four more candidates.

Annette flopped on to the nearest barre. Her hands were shaking, partly through nerves, partly through sheer exhaustion.

Someone opened the door and announced that there were cups of tea in the girls' dressing-room, if anyone wanted one. Annette accepted thankfully. She had only had time for a cup of tea and a sandwich at lunch-time, in spite of what she had said to Angus, and for breakfast – she tried to remember what she had had for breakfast, then realised with a shock that it was at breakfast that she'd heard the awful news about Black Bess. She could hardly believe it. It seemed years ago – another world!

'How do you think you did?' someone asked her. As if she knew! As if she'd have told them, even if she did know.

'Oh, so-so,' she answered non-committally. In her heart of hearts, she hoped for the best. She hadn't made any ghastly mistakes, anyway.

Miss Brandon appeared at the door. 'How did you manage to get here, Annette?' she asked. Miss Brandon, like everybody else, had heard all about the floods. When Annette told her, she looked grave. 'In fact, I wonder you were able to dance at all, my dear,' she said.

It was then that Annette knew just how tired she was. The room swung round her, and she clutched at the mantelshelf to steady herself.

'Yes, I am a bit tired,' she said faintly. 'I-I think I'll sit down.'

'You're going home tonight?' questioned Miss Brandon.

Annette considered. She'd never even thought about it.

'I don't expect I can,' she said. 'The road may not be open yet. But Aunt Molly will let me stay here, though she won't be expecting me. I shall have to get home tomorrow, though, because school starts on Wednesday and I haven't got my things, my school uniform and my books, I mean.'

11   THE PLANS O' MICE AND MEN

Waiting for the results of her exam was rather like a prisoner waiting for the jury to consider their verdict, thought Annette, as she tried to keep her mind on her lessons. She hadn't gone home, after all. Mrs Dancy had sent her school things, all packed into a large suitcase, on the Tuesday bus, which had managed to get through the flooded area by one of the loop-roads. Tucked into the folds of her gym-tunic was a letter which Annette pulled out eagerly. Mrs Dancy always enclosed a letter with her parcels, remembering from her own childhood how disappointing it is to open a package with not even a note inside. She wrote as follows:

Dancing Peel.
Tuesday.

My darling,
We were all thinking about you yesterday at two o'clock, and wondering how you were getting on, and whether you would manage to be in time, so it was a great

relief when Angus rang up to say you'd caught the bus at Bellingham, and when you rang up to say everything was all right.

Angus rode back early this morning, and neither he nor his pony seem any the worse for their adventure. I do think it was very sweet of him to help you out like that, and I hope you weren't thinking so much about your exam that you forgot to thank him. He really is a dear boy!

Now for some news! Max is bringing your case with your school things into Newcastle on the two o'clock bus, and he isn't going back to school himself. He's joining Teresa and Luisillo and their Company of Spanish Dancers straight away, and he's travelling to London by the midnight train tomorrow, so you'll be able to see him off. I'm not as dismayed as you might think, because I knew in my heart that this would happen sooner or later.

The flood is subsiding, though it will take many months – perhaps years – to repair the damage. They have managed to patch up Callow bridge, so that the buses can get through. Poor old Sally Muirhead woke up yesterday morning to find her kitchen a foot or more deep in water, and Timmy and the kitten floating on the top in their basket! Although I believe it's a fact that cats can swim quite well if they have to, I expect it doesn't apply to three-legged ones!

Well, darling, perhaps you will be able to come home this weekend and tell me all the news. You may know the results of your exam by then. Anyway, I expect I haven't packed all the things you want. Angus is off to school on Saturday. It seems a strange day to go, but I suppose the idea is to get settled in before Monday. You'll just see him before he goes.

With lots of love to Aunt Molly and yourself,

Mummy.

P.S. Bella was a tower of strength! Although she knew I couldn't pay her any wages, she insisted on staying all day and helping to get rid of all the water. Angus came next morning and would scrub the kitchen floor for me, and Max set to and cleaned all the shoes and boots in the house – no mean task, because they were all caked with mud. He even cleaned the wellingtons! Everyone was so kind, it almost made it worth while having a flood!

It will seem very quiet when Max has gone to London. I've always been preparing for the weekend, or half-term, when the two of you would be back. But never mind – I still have a daughter left, haven't I?

Love again, Mummy.

Sometimes Annette went home to Aunt Molly's flat directly after school, had a meal, and then dashed off to her ballet class, fitting in her homework as best she could. This Friday, however, she caught the bus to Rothbury Crescent at the school gates, and went straight to Miss Brandon's. You never knew – the exam results might be out. She couldn't bear to wait!

The studios were dark when she got there. The ordinary classes hadn't begun yet, and the ballet students weren't due to arrive for another half an hour. She could do a bit of barre work to fill in the time.

It was while she was taking her tights and tunic out of her case that she heard a voice from Miss Brandon's flat, which was above the school. Evidently Miss Brandon was talking to someone on the telephone. Annette didn't deliberately eavesdrop, but it was impossible not to hear a stray sentence or two. Then, after a lot of talk about the Christmas pantomime, Miss Brandon's voice said casually, 'By the way – did I tell you the results of the Elementary RAD exam? No, I thought not. Well, it was highly satisfactory. They all got through, except little Annette Dancy. Failed by one mark. I'm afraid she'll

be very disappointed, poor child, but really, when you think of what she went through, all that flood, and on horseback, it isn't surprising . . . oh, just a moment! Hold the line will you? I've got a bit of surprising news for you . . . Shan't be a minute!'

Annette didn't wait to hear more. Failed by one mark! The words rang in her ears. All her castles in the air tumbled about her. All her dreams, her bright, glittering dreams of taking London by storm, faded. Tears streamed down her cheeks. Sobs shook her. As she made her way to the bus-stop, people turned round and stared at her, wondering what was wrong with the child with the tragic white face. But Annette didn't even see them. All she thought about was getting home; somewhere where she could be alone in her misery.

It's odd how short a time it takes for one's whole world to change, thought Annette sadly. Why, the very same bus she had come on was still waiting at the bus-station. Yet, while it stood there, Annette Dancy's career had collapsed. More than that, it was now quite certain that her mother would have to leave their peel-tower home and go out and work. She, Annette, would have to give up her dream of being a dancer, and learn to be something ordinary. Something sensible, thought Annette with a sob of self-pity, like a schoolteacher, or perhaps she would go into a shop. Yes, it had better be a shop, she decided bitterly. Then she could at least sell ballet-shoes, even if she couldn't dance in them!

'Hello, missie – you back again?' said the bus-driver, giving her a friendly wink. 'What's the matter, kid? It'll all be the same in a 'undred years time! What's up, now? Tell your Uncle George.' The man obviously thought she was about twelve years old! 'I'll bet you forgot to do your homework.'

'My goodness! I *have*!' exclaimed Annette. 'At least, I haven't forgotten to do it – I've left it in the dressing-room.'

The man clucked through his teeth at her in mock disapproval.

'Only just in time, aren't you,' he said, ringing the bell for departure. 'Good luck, miss, and cheer up, do. Christmas is coming, never fear!'

Annette flung herself off the bus again. Troubles never came singly. Now she would have to wait for the next bus, and by that time her fellow students would be arriving and she didn't want to meet them. How could she meet them? They'd all passed. Her pride was in the dust! She dashed back to the ballet-school and up the stairs to the dressing-room. Perhaps there was just time to snatch up her things before anyone arrived.

But her luck was out. Miss Brandon herself stood in the lobby outside the big studio.

'Oh, hello, Annette,' she said cheerfully. 'Come in, dear. I want to talk to you.' She beckoned Annette into the studio and shut the door.

Annette's tears began to fall again.

'It's all right, Miss Brandon,' she gulped. 'I know

all about it. I heard you on the telephone. I failed by one mark. Oh, how miserable I am! What an idiot I am ever to think that I could dance!' Great sobs shook her.

'But you can dance, my dear,' said Miss Brandon's quiet voice, and there was a hint of laughter in it. 'Just because you fail an RAD exam doesn't mean –'

'Oh, don't try to soften it!' broke in Annette. 'It's very kind of you, but I can't bear it! I know the worst now. You see, I heard what you said. "Poor Annette," you said, "I'm afraid she will be very disappointed . . ."'

'If you had waited just a little longer, Annette,' put in Miss Brandon quietly, 'you would have heard me telling Miss Littleton another rather surprising bit of news – the news that, although a certain Annette Dancy had failed to pass her exam by one mark, due, no doubt, to her exhausting ride through the storm, yet this same Annette had excited the interest of one of the examiners, a very important one, too.' She mentioned a name that made Annette gasp. 'Although he quite agreed with the other examiner that you were not quite up to the standard required by the RAD technically, yet he felt – as I do, Annette – that one day you will, barring accidents, be a great dancer. So he has offered you a place in his London school connected with the Cosmopolitan Ballet Company. It is a scholarship, and not only your dancing lessons will be paid for, but your board and lodging as well. Mr Reinholt knows your circumstances. All you will have to do will be to work hard, and that, Annette, I am sure you will do. Mr Reinholt believes in you so much that he is offering you this. As for your failure in the RAD exam – well,' added Miss Brandon with a smile, 'I have had failures before, and some of them have still succeeded, and have become members and soloists, and even prima ballerinas, of famous companies. You have heard of Alicia Browne?'

'Yes, of course; everyone has,' said Annette with a hiccup.

'Well, she was one of my pupils,' said Miss Brandon. 'Her name was not Alicia Browne in those days. 'It was –' Miss Brandon smiled a little at the thought of her distinguished pupil's absurd name '– it was Alice Bott. Of course she had to change it! Well, you see, Alice failed her Elementary RAD exam by one mark. Just like you, Annette!'

'Oh, I'm so happy, darling, darling Miss Brandon!' cried Annette, throwing her arms round her dancing-mistress. 'A moment ago I was so miserable, I felt I should like to die. And now I'm so h-happy!'

'Well, don't cry about it,' said Miss Brandon, but there were tears in her own eyes. She couldn't help sharing in the joys and griefs of her pupils, and she loved this one very dearly. 'Surely you've cried enough for one day! I think a very good idea would be to put in some practise on your petits battements. Your RAD report said: "petits battements weak", and, you know, I feel the report is right. So, if you have time before your bus –'

'I have!' said Annette, blowing her nose. 'I'll practise them till I drop!'

She danced out of the studio and put on her tights. Let her fellow students come and exult in their petty triumphs! What did Annette care? She wouldn't change places with any of them. She'd got her chance. She was going to be a great dancer – Mr Reinholt had said so! There was no false modesty about Annette when it was a question of dancing!

12 EPILOGUE

And now it is time to say goodbye to Dancing Peel. The sun has set over the flooded landscape, the moors have turned blue, then purple, the stars have come out. The Border country lies peacefully under the round, yellow harvest moon. Even the old peel-tower has lost something of its grim aspect, and you feel it is blessing the two young figures who stand upon its flat roof in the frosty moonlight.

'Annette,' said Angus suddenly, for there had been silence between them for quite a while. 'What was it you were going to tell me the day we rode through the flood – something about my pony?'

'I was very wicked,' said Annette gravely. 'I let poor Black Bess out of her stable in that awful storm, and – and – I did it on purpose, Angus!'

'You did, did you? Well, may I be asking you why you did so?'

'It was what you said about wanting us to leave Dancing Peel.'

'Wanting you to leave Dancing Peel?' repeated Angus. 'What is this you are saying, Annette?'

216

'But you said,' persisted Annette, 'Sheena said –'

'Ah! Now we are coming to it. What words, exactly, did Sheena put into my mouth?'

Annette thought long and deeply.

'Well, she didn't say exactly what you said, Angus. But she –'

'She made you think that I said them?'

'Yes.'

'And are you always taking for the truth whatever Sheena is saying?'

Annette was silent.

'You are understanding, Annette?'

'I – I think so. You mean what Sheena said was not true? Or at least what she meant me to think was not true?'

'That is correct.'

'Then – then you don't want us to leave the peel? Oh, Angus, and I've been worrying and worrying about it.'

'You are being very stupid, Annette, and very foolish, too. If you had told me about this before, I could have explained. You see, at first my father did not know how hard your mother found it to make ends meet. We thought you were quite well off. Then we heard about you not employing Bella any more, and also about your ballet dress. It all added up, and we talked things over, and now my father has got a plan. He has even discussed it with the diocesan architect, but until he knew how your mother felt, he could not do anything more about it.'

'What sort of a plan, Angus?' said Annette, a faint gleam of hope entering her heart. Angus and his father were such strong, solid people. Perhaps they really could help.

'A plan to divide the peel,' said Angus. 'When Max is not there and you are gone to London, your mother would be very lonely in this large old house – even if she could afford still to live here. Yet we all know how much she loves it, how she would hate to live anywhere else. But if it were divided, my father and I could live in one part, and your mother in another. The architect thinks it would even divide into three, and there would be room for another family.'

'Oh, Angus, I think it's a perfectly heavenly idea!' cried Annette.

'You would not mind sharing your home with us?'

'Of course not,' said Annette.

'But I remember at one time you did not like to share even your stable with me?'

'That was a long time ago,' declared Annette.

'Then that is all right,' said Angus.

There was silence between them again for a few minutes. Then Angus said, 'If we were living in a book, I expect our parents would fall in love and get married.'

'Oh, no!' said Annette. 'Why, they're old!'

'Not exactly!' laughed Angus. 'Your mother is not quite forty, I think, and my father is forty-five. But you need not sound so shocked, because I do not think it will happen. If your father was the sort of person your mother loved, then she would not love the sort of person *my* father is, would she? They are so very different. Besides –'

He stopped suddenly.

'Yes? Besides, what?' prompted Annette.

'I am thinking about my own mother,' he went on. 'She was little and slender, with big dark eyes – rather like you, Annette – and she had a funny little way of ruffling up her hair when she tried to add up the accounts and always got them wrong. It's strange how you remember the little things about people you love when – when they are not there.'

'Was she ill for a long time?' asked Annette. 'Or was it an awful shock when she died, like Daddy? He caught pneumonia, and died in two days. I was only five, so I don't remember much about it, but Mummy told me.'

'My mother was not ill at all,' said Angus. 'She died in a climbing accident only last year. She was a great rock-climber was my mother. We were all climbing in the Black Cuillin and on that particular day we were negotiating a tricky bit of climbing on a rocky ledge between Sgurr Alasdair and Sgurr Sgumain. We were roped together; my mother was leading. She fell, and my father would have held her, but the rope was cut on a sharp razor-edge of rock. She was killed before our eyes.'

'Oh, Angus, I'm so sorry!' The boy could hear

the tears in the girl's voice. 'Poor, poor, Angus!'

'My father loved her very deeply,' went on Angus. 'I know that he still does. So, as I say, since we are not living in a book, but in real life, he will stay a widower. In real life things do not always end quite happily ever after, as they say in fairy stories.'

'No – not for you,' agreed Annette. 'But for me everything is wonderful! Thanks to Mr Reinholt, and my scholarship, and Max's contract with Teresa and Luisillo and her Company, and now your father's idea about Dancing Peel . . . Mummy will be able to stay here, and I shan't feel she's lonely, either.'

'Do you realise, Annette, that the next time we meet, we shall be living here all together under one roof? At least, we shall if they've managed to get the dividing done.'

'Yes, what fun it will be!'

'So, for the present, this is goodbye, Annette.' He held out his hand.

'Oh,' said Annette, 'but I thought you weren't going until tomorrow.'

'I am riding over to Coldburn tonight, and tomorrow they are taking me over to my school in the car.'

'Oh, Angus, wait a minute! There's something else I want to tell you. I want us to be friends, Angus – not just a truce between us. You understand?'

'I am understanding, Annette. There is to be peace between you and me in spite of our different ways of thinking. That is what you are meaning?'

'Yes. Although some of the things you do are all wrong, I still can't help liking you. So goodbye, Angus, and thank you for everything.'

They shook hands solemnly, and a moment later he was gone. Annette was alone with only the stars and the moon for company. A few minutes later she heard the faint clip-clop of horse's hoofs on the road, and she knew that Angus was on his way.

'I wonder what's in store for me when I go south?' said Annette to herself.

The stars winked, and the yellow moon looked down on her serenely. Perhaps they knew, only they weren't telling!